The Air I Breathe

STEADFAST LOVE BOOK 1

By Karen Baney

The Air I Breathe: Steadfast Love Book 1
By Karen Baney

Publisher:
Desert Life Media, LLC
Gilbert, AZ 85295

www.karenbaney.com

Printed in the United States of America

ISBN 978-1-960217-05-9

Thus says the Lord God to these bones: "Behold, I will cause breath to enter you, and you shall live. And I will lay sinews upon you, and will cause flesh to come upon you, and cover you with skin, and put breath in you, and you shall live, and you shall know that I am the Lord."

— Ezekiel 37:5-6

1

Kelly

"ALANA, COME ON." Kelly failed to keep the frustration from her voice as she pulled a fresh shirt and leggings from her six-year-old daughter's closet.

"I don't like that shirt." Alana crossed her arms over her chest as her lower lip curled downward. Her dark hair flopped in her eyes.

"Which shirt would you like to wear?" Kelly kept the edge out of her voice that time, even though her patience wore thin at the third attempt to dress her daughter.

"The blue one with the unicorn."

"It's in the dirty clothes basket."

Alana huffed, crossing her arms over her chest.

"How about this one?"

"Fine." Alana's arms went limp, but her scowl stayed.

Kelly sucked in a deep breath as she helped Alana into the yellow shirt and matching leggings. She tossed her daughter a pair of socks and asked her to tie her shoes before going downstairs for breakfast.

Then Kelly hurried back into her room, removed her robe, and donned a light pink blouse. As she tucked it into her high-waisted jeans, she opened her makeup drawer. Taking less than ten minutes, she applied a thin foundation, concealer, powder, and mascara. No time for anything more colorful. She donned no-show socks before stuffing her feet into a pair of checkered Vans. As she stood in front of the mirror, she surveyed her appearance. Presentable. Almost.

Good enough for a single mom.

Once she finished, she hurried down to the kitchen. After she filled a bowl with Alana's favorite cereal, she poured milk over it. The brightly colored crispies popped in the cool liquid.

"Mom! I wanted Reese puffs!"

Too late. "Here, eat this."

Alana tapped the spoon against the bar, her eyes flashing defiantly. The sound of the metal on the granite countertop reverberated through the room, grating on Kelly's nerves.

"Alana." Kelly glared at her daughter, wondering when had she become so willful.

Slowly, Alana ate the soggy cereal.

Kelly let out a sigh as she opened the fridge. She tore the foil top off a yogurt and scarfed it down before she glanced at the clock. The daycare asked her to arrive by seven-thirty. She would not make it.

"Come on, sweetie. Let's go."

Alana stuffed one last bite into her mouth as Kelly held out her coat. After she slid her arms into the sleeves, she zipped it up herself. At least she stopped fussing about every little thing.

Until they arrived at daycare.

"Why can't I stay home with you?"

"Because I have to look for a job. I might interview if things work out. And school doesn't start until after New Year's."

"Mommy, I don't want to go to daycare."

Too bad. She bit back the words and forced a cheerier tone. "It will be fun. You'll meet some new girls your age."

She cut the engine on her beat up Corolla. Then she opened the back door and unfastened Alana's seatbelt.

Alana swatted at her. "I can do it!"

Kelly withdrew her hand. Once Alana climbed out of the car, Kelly held her daughter's hand until they entered the building. Then Alana pulled away.

"Morning Mrs. Sutton," the daycare center receptionist greeted her with a strained smile.

"Miss," Kelly corrected.

With a glare, the woman gave a quick, affirmative nod. Kelly clamped her mouth shut, fighting the urge to release a harsh retort. It was the twenty-first century. Plenty of single parents must use their daycare. She couldn't be the only single mom dropping off a child.

"This must be Alana."

Kelly nodded. The woman's voice was firm as she rattled off the rules and asked for an alternate contact.

"Her father, Kyle Jacobs, may pick her up sometimes. And possibly her aunt, Marcy Schaefer." Kelly pulled up the contacts on her phone and jotted down their numbers.

"If anyone else needs to fill in, you or her father will need to notify us ahead of time."

"Understood."

The woman gave her a copy of the paperwork, which Kelly crammed into her large everyday canvas purse. She thanked her, then hugged Alana tightly. The sweet, un-mistakable bubblegum scent of her body wash lingered.

"I'll be back at three. Or your daddy will pick you up at five if I can't make it."

"Love you, Mommy."

"Love you, sweetie."

Kelly waved as a worker introduced Alana to the other six-year-olds. Then she strode out to the parking lot and climbed into her car. Letting out a loud sigh, she rested her head on the steering wheel.

What had she been thinking, uprooting her life to move to Chandler, Arizona? It certainly seemed to make sense when Kyle suggested it a few weeks ago during a visit with Alana.

Yeah, that whole thing still felt weird. Her baby's daddy, Kyle, had finally stepped up to be a father about a year ago after he found Jesus. Kelly was glad he wanted to be a part of Alana's life, even though it made Kelly's more complicated.

They had been friends once, back in college. Though she planned to save intimacy for marriage, she failed. Because she had been so desperate to feel loved by someone — anyone — she allowed things to go too far with Kyle. One night changed her life forever.

A tear slid down her cheek at the memory. When she first told Kyle she was pregnant, he distanced himself, agreeing to pay child support and nothing more. She lost her only friend and became a single mom.

As Kelly squared her shoulders, she sent a quick prayer of gratitude heavenward that Kyle wanted to be a part of Alana's life now. Even though they shared zero romantic interest in each other, she and Kyle's friendship had rekindled. It was good for them to find a way to co-parent their daughter, for Alana's sake. Truthfully, he had been a godsend as he helped them move to Chandler, Arizona, a few days ago. It had been his idea for them to move closer to where he lived so he could be more involved in Alana's life. Kelly had been brokenhearted after her fiancé ended their engagement and she had lost her job, so she impulsively moved.

Now she was in a new city, jobless and mostly alone. Letting out a loud breath, she turned on her car and the roar of the engine broke through the silence. No time for a breakdown. She needed to find a job.

Kelly's stomach tightened as she pulled into the parking lot of her townhouse. Memories of her breakup with her fiancé raced through her mind. Derek, the low-life, broke up with her over text message while she had been in Arizona for Kyle's sister's wedding. When she had returned to Colorado Springs, Derek admitted he had been seeing someone else for months. How she ended up engaged to a cheating man, she did not know. But those were Derek's true colors. At least she found it out *before* she married the jerk.

The conversation when he picked up the ring still crushed her heart. He didn't want to wait until marriage to be intimate. He had glanced at Alana and made some comment about how Kelly's old-fashioned convictions must not have been important to her almost seven years ago. Otherwise, she wouldn't have been a single mom.

As Kelly opened the door to the townhouse—the one Kyle owned and graciously let her live in rent-free until she found a new job—she dropped her purse on the kitchen counter. She tidied up the kitchen from the hurried breakfast. The spoon clanked against the dirty cereal bowl as she loaded them into the dishwasher.

When she finished, she sat on one of the bar stools staring at the job website on her laptop. The quiet of the house failed to calm her nerves. She typed in a search for event coordinator positions and drummed her fingers on the cool granite, waiting for the results to load.

At twenty-nine, her life turned out far differently than she dreamed. Starting over on her own as a single mom in a strange new city wasn't what she expected. She had hoped to be married. To raise a family.

Instead, she was living in a townhouse owned by her baby's daddy while she started over again. She couldn't live off his charity forever. She needed a job. A job when the hospitality industry struggled to restart after a few tough years. The week between Christmas and New Year's was a terrible time to look.

When she stood, the tightness in her chest started. Her eyes widened as her breathing morphed into wheezing. Lightheadedness overwhelmed her, and she fell to her knees, the coolness of the tile floor seeping through her pants. As she reached for her purse on the bar, it crashed to the floor, littering its contents everywhere. She found her phone and tapped the picture of Kyle's face. She couldn't draw in a breath of air. Then she sat on her legs and bent

forward to keep from passing out. Her heart raced frantic-
ally.

"Kelly?"

"Need." Gulp of air. "Help."

"Is it happening?"

"Yes."

"I'll send someone right away."

The line went dead. Her vision swam as her lungs
constricted. *Please God.*

2

Matt

As Matt Dixon turned off the shower, he heard his phone ringing. He wiped the water from his hand and tucked a towel around his waist as he answered the phone.

"Kyle, what's up?"

"Have you left yet?"

"No. Still at home."

A loud exhale came across the line. "It's Kelly."

Kelly? Who was Kelly?

"I called 911. Go now!"

"What—"

"The key is on my dresser. As the landlord, you have my permission to enter."

The cool air in the bathroom tickled Matt's damp back as his mind spun. Oh! Kelly was the mother of Kyle's daughter. The one that just moved to town.

"She can't be alone. It makes everything worse when she is."

"What are you talking about?" Matt's heart raced and his hands tingled over the urgency in his roommate's voice.

"Go! And Matt?"

"Yeah."

"Pray."

The line went dead. He stared at it for half a second before he leaped into motion. He swabbed the soft towel across his body. Then he scrubbed it over his dripping hair before dropping it on the floor. He turned and donned his clothes as quickly as he could. As he rushed past his bed, he grabbed his Bible.

When Matt jumped in his car, he took a quick second to text his boss that he wouldn't be in today. Then he backed out of the garage, praying as he drove.

Lord, I don't know what's going on, but You do. Please be with Kelly. He realized he did not know what her last name was. It didn't matter. God knew who he meant. *Help her. Let the paramedics get to her in time. Show me what to do.*

As he pulled into the closest visitor's spot to the townhouse, he turned his car off. Then he grabbed his Bible and fished the house key from his pocket. He didn't waste time knocking on the door. Instead, he unlocked it and hurried inside. He tossed his Bible and the key on the bar.

"Kelly?"

She didn't acknowledge him as she remained on the floor, folded over her knees. A jolt of fear shot through him at her dreadful wheezing. *Lord. Please help.*

"It's me, Matt."

When he kneeled beside her, her clammy hand clasped his like a vise grip. He rubbed his other hand in circles on her back. He felt her muscles tighten through the thin blouse. How else could he comfort her?

"Kyle sent me over. I'm his roommate."

The air felt heavy as her ragged gasps of air filled the room, causing his throat to constrict.

"Remember, we met at Marcy's wedding?"

When she didn't respond, he continued to rub her back.

"The ambulance is on the way."

"No." Her barely audible protest was so weak, a mere whisper flanked by her jagged breathing.

"Kyle already called them. I... I think it's good they are coming. They'll know what to do."

She swayed as she tried to sit up. The fear in her dark brown eyes pierced his heart. Tears streamed down her face. Then she doubled over again.

"Paramedics!" a man's deep voice bellowed from the open door.

"In here!" Matt replied as he let out a loud breath.

The male medic rushed to Kelly's side and took her pulse, while the female medic bombarded Matt with a flurry of questions. The muscles in his shoulders tensed with each one.

"What happened?"

"I... I'm not sure. I'm her... My roommate called me. He's the one that called you."

"Panic. Attack."

Kelly spit out the words as the male EMT helped her sit upright. She leaned back, resting her head against the wall of the bar. Then he hooked her up to the mobile oxygen tank while Matt stared in shock.

"Does this happen often?" The woman asked.

"I don't know. Maybe."

Kyle seemed to know what was happening when he called Matt. He curled his finger and bounced the knuckle against his upper lip. His gaze darted to the open door and back to the female EMT before it settled on Kelly's face. Her skin faded from purple to red, then to skin tone. Her chest rose and fell with normal breathing. Matt breathed slower, too.

When she ripped the oxygen mask off her face, the medic frowned.

"Ma'am, we'd like to take you for observation to make sure you're alright."

"No. Need." She took a steady breath. "Panic attack is over. I'll be fine."

"Do you take any anti-anxiety medication? Have you worked with your primary care physician?"

She narrowed her eyes before she answered. "No. I don't take any medication. My doctor did not recommend it."

Then her eyes darted away. Matt wondered if she had

ever asked her doctor about it.

The woman EMT crouched down next to her. "We strongly recommend coming with us."

Kelly vehemently shook her head. "I'm fine now. Just tired."

The woman turned to Matt. "Well, we can't force her if she declines treatment. Will you be around for a while? Just in case?"

"Yes. I'll stay with her."

The woman studied him for a moment before they left, closing the door behind them.

He felt the chill of the tile floor seep through his clothing as he slid down to sit across from Kelly. She gave him a weak smile.

"You don't have to stay. I'll be fine."

Matt hitched a shoulder. "I skipped work when Kyle called."

She grimaced, then her chin dipped to her chest. "I'm sorry he dragged you into this."

"Would you like something to drink?" he asked.

"Water."

He stood and opened cupboards until he found a glass. After he filled it with water from the filtered water spigot in the fridge door, he handed it to her. She sipped the drink.

"Does that happen often?" he asked softly as he sat on the floor again.

"From time to time."

"What causes it?"

"Stress. Panic. Feeling overwhelmed."

"Like starting over in a new city?"

She quirked a half-smile as red colored her cheeks. "Like that."

Matt studied her as she sipped the water. She had changed her hairstyle since Marcy's wedding. Odd that he noticed it. He had only met her that one time. Danced one dance. He liked the shorter style. It suited her.

When her gaze found his, he cleared his throat. Then he stood and retrieved his Bible.

"Mind if I read to you for a few minutes?"

She nodded.

He took a seat in a chair at the small table nearby. Once he flipped open to Psalm 121, he read it aloud. "I lift up my eyes to the hills. From where does my help come? My help comes from the Lord, who made heaven and earth. He will not let your foot be moved; he who keeps you will not slumber... The Lord will keep your going out and your coming in from this time forth and forevermore."

When he glanced up, Kelly leaned her head against the wall and closed her eyes. She was beautiful, despite the ordeal. Her dark brown hair framed her face, curling slightly below her chin. Her narrow nose elongated her face, drawing attention to her perfectly pink lips. His gaze fixed on them for a few seconds. Then he forced himself to look away.

He needed to leave, but compassion rooted him in place. Clearly, Kelly would benefit from a listening ear and a prayerful heart. He knew that was the main reason Kyle had called him. Matt would make the time to help any hurting soul, beyond just comforting her in the crisis.

He rubbed a hand on the back of his neck.

"Would you like to join me for coffee?"

"I would love some if you're driving."

He chuckled. "Of course."

After he closed his Bible, he helped her up. She shoved the contents of her purse back in it. Then the two of them headed out.

Matt held the car door open for her before he rounded to the other side. When he climbed in, he reached behind her and dropped his things on the back seat. A whiff of strawberries floated up to his nose, causing him to breathe a little deeper. The simple and sweet fragrance fit her.

"Any preference?" he asked.

"One with a secluded table might be nice."

Her response caused his chest to expand. He reminded himself he suggested coffee to help her. Not because he couldn't bring himself to leave her yet.

3

Kelly

AS MATT DROVE them to a coffee shop, Kelly studied him. She remembered him from the wedding. They danced once or twice. The thing that stood out to her then, and again now, was his kind heart and calm demeanor. He oozed peace, something she rarely experienced. She wanted to spend more time around him for that reason alone.

"That Psalm. It was one of the Psalms of Ascent, wasn't it?" she asked.

He quirked an eyebrow before he answered. "Yes. Psalm 121."

"I lift up my eyes... What did it say about slumber again?"

"He who keeps you will not slumber."

"Hmm. I guess I need to remember that God is taking care of me."

God knew her situation. He wasn't asleep or distant or uncaring. He knew she needed a job. And He provided Kyle's help with a roof over her head. And He sent Matt so she wouldn't be alone during a panic attack.

With a deep, calming breath, she closed her eyes and breathed in God's comfort. The spicy scent of Matt's cologne brought a smile to her lips as she exhaled slowly. He smelled like home. Not that it made any sense.

"Here we are," he said as he pulled into a parking spot.

"Thank you. I can't tell you how much it means that you showed up and helped me."

He snorted. "I'm not sure I did much to help."

"More than you know."

Matt got out of the car and opened the door for her, the cool air chilling her. She slid from the seat and stood with the door between them. Kelly smiled, hoping her gratitude came across sincerely.

For a moment, they just lingered there, feeling the warmth of the sun on her face. He stood a few inches taller than her, a rarity. His hazel eyes radiated a calming peace, mirroring the serenity she experienced in his presence. With her purse in hand, she stepped back from the door and heard the creak of the hinges as he slowly closed it.

Once inside, they ordered their coffees. Matt waited for them while Kelly found a seat. There was a section of the L-shaped coffee shop that offered more privacy. Thankfully, a table remained open. She sat and dropped her purse on the floor as the soft sound of smooth jazz floated above her. The aroma of freshly ground coffee permeated the air, renewing her energy and causing her mouth to water. A few minutes later, Matt joined her.

Sliding into the chair across from her, he asked, "So, what's making you anxious?"

"You mean besides moving to a new city where I only know my baby's daddy?"

"Yeah, besides that."

Clearly, Matt must have known the story about her and Kyle. They were roommates, and Kyle had sent him. Matt hadn't seemed to judge her—yet.

"The last month has been overwhelming. My fiancé dumped me while I was in town for Marcy's wedding. We dated for a year and were engaged for six months."

"I'm sorry. That must have been heartbreaking."

"Even more so when he told me he was seeing someone else."

Matt's expression darkened, and he kept his mouth closed as his jaw ticked.

"When I returned to Colorado, I learned that the resort I worked for had decreased its staff, and I was among those let go. Since I had no job and no family there and only a few friends, it made sense to move here. At least I'd have help with Alana now that Kyle has stepped up to be a father to her."

As he sipped his coffee, her eyes dropped to the one in her hands. She turned it around on the table, causing the sweet caramel aroma to waft. Finally, she took a swig before she continued.

"Most of my friends from church blamed me for the end of my engagement. Guess no one cared to hear the truth."

She held back a snort, knowing it wouldn't be the last time she encountered hypocrites. She and her mother faced similar resentment when the story broke about her father. How people could blame the victims instead of the offender never made sense to her.

Kelly took another sip of the sweet, frothy drink to stall as the truth dawned on her. Derek had been far too much like her father. Broken promises. Secrets. Dodgy behavior. Excuses. Pressuring her to be something different from who she was.

As her chest constricted, a wheezing sound came from her throat. Her vision narrowed and the music overhead muffled. She closed her eyes while she placed her palms flat against the smooth tabletop. Breathe in. Breathe out.

Matt's warm hands, with their comforting strength, settled over hers. Calmly spoken words helped her focus on her breathing.

"I lift my eyes up... He never sleeps nor slumbers..."

Slowly, life-giving air filled the bottom of her lungs. When she opened her eyes, her heart rate slowed. Matt's eyebrows drew together above his intense hazel eyes. As he squeezed her hands, his features softened.

"You don't have to tell me if it's too much."

Kelly pulled her hands away and offered an awkward

smile as her gaze drifted to her coffee cup. "I'll be fine."

Then a strangled attempt at a laugh escaped her lips. "It's been years since I've had a panic attack. Now twice in one morning."

"It sounds like you've been through a lot."

Her head bobbed slightly as she exhaled loudly. "I have. And I need to stop dwelling on it. Start looking forward. Start rebuilding my life."

Matt studied her over the rim of his coffee cup. "I assume you're looking for a position as an event coordinator?"

"Yes. So far I haven't found much."

"Have you considered the resort down at Wild Horse Pass?"

She shook her head. "Where is that?"

"It's only about fifteen or twenty minutes from here on the rez. It's a five-star hotel. I know the resort manager."

"A five-star hotel on the rez?" She quirked an eyebrow.

"A pro football team stayed there the last time the championship game was in town."

"Really?"

Matt withdrew his phone and typed out a quick message. A few seconds later, his phone dinged.

"My friend Dwight says he would love to talk with you. What's your number and I'll send you his contact info?"

Kelly created a new contact for 'Matt' and handed her phone to him. He typed in his last name and number. Then sent a text to himself before he texted her back with Dwight's info.

"What's your last name?" he asked.

"Sutton."

"He says you should reach out today to set up something for tomorrow."

"Tomorrow? So soon?"

"Too soon?"

"No. No. That would be wonderful."

Kelly scarcely believed how much Matt helped her, a stranger. First, with the panic attack in her home. Now with a lead for a new job. Such a kind man. So different from anyone she knew.

After she took another sip of her coffee, she said, "Tell me something about yourself. I'm tired of talking about me."

Matt smiled as he leaned forward. "What would you like to know?"

"How did you meet Kyle?"

"His sister, Marcy, has been in my home group for a few years. When Kyle moved to the area, she dragged him along."

Home group. Kelly's stomach tightened, and her skin pricked at the mixed feelings the words stirred. She longed for those friendships. Yet, memories from her teen years held her back. When she let people get too close, they betrayed her. She couldn't risk being hurt like that again.

"We meet on Wednesdays."

"Is that so?"

She shifted in the hard wooden chair. She needed friends. Others like Matt that would care about her and listen to her. Maybe this time would be different.

"You're welcome to join us."

"I'll think about it."

It might be awkward going to Kyle's home group. Or it just might be good for Alana to see both her parents trying to build friendships and their faith. Maybe with Kyle, Marcy, and Matt there, no one would stab her in the back this time.

As she downed the last of her coffee, she stood and asked Matt to take her home. She had monopolized enough of his time.

4

Matt

MATT HOPED HE hadn't overstepped with his invitation to home group. He couldn't read Kelly's reaction. Apart from the fact that she and Kyle had a daughter, and that she had recently moved to Arizona, he was clueless about her past. But he sensed she needed friends. Christian friends.

Always the true gentleman, he held the car door open for her. Once she buckled up, he settled behind the wheel and pulled out of the parking lot.

"What do you do for a living?" she asked.

"I'm a financial analyst for a chip manufacturer. Part of my job is to calculate the potential return on investment. Crunch a bunch of numbers with lots of assumptions."

"Sounds riveting."

He laughed. "It's not. It's what they trained me to do, and it pays the bills. My genuine passion…"

When he glanced over at Kelly, he saw her expectant expression. He considered opening up. If she joined his home group, she would find out fairly quickly, anyway.

"I'm going to seminary at night and I work part-time at our church. An internship with the youth ministry."

Kelly stiffened in her seat. Her voice sounded unnaturally cheery. "That's amazing."

His shoulders slumped. Her false enthusiasm was not the reaction he hoped for.

"When do you finish?"

"May."

"Ah, so you're in the home stretch then. It must be nice to see the end in sight."

Matt straightened as he pulled into a parking spot outside of her place. "I'm looking forward to the next chapter wherever God leads."

She nodded slowly as he turned off his car.

His hand froze on his door handle. He sensed her hesitation, so he folded his hands in his lap and waited.

"My father was a pastor."

Matt blinked at her whispered confession. When he shifted toward her, she bowed her head. Her hair hid her face as she turned her shoulders away from him. His heart ached for her obvious pain.

Then Kelly wiped her fingers under her eyes. With a forced laugh, she said, "Thank goodness for waterproof mascara."

Suddenly, she reached for the handle and shoved the car door open. The hinges groaned in protest. She sniffed before she ducked down to make eye contact.

"Thanks for all your help today."

After he called her name, he asked, "Would you like me to pray with you?"

Her eyes darted to her home, then back to him as she bit her lower lip.

He held his breath for a few seconds, praying she would accept his offer. Clearly, she needed to take her hurt to the Lord. If he could help by praying on her behalf, then he would.

She slid back into the seat, her back sinking into the cushion with a sigh. "I suppose it wouldn't hurt."

When he held his hands out, palms up, she placed hers in them. Then he bowed his head and prayed.

"Lord, we ask for your wisdom and discernment as Kelly applies for a new job. Help her lean on you as she adjusts to her new life. We know you brought her here for her good. Not just her daughter's."

And heal her brokenness. Help her trust me. Give her the courage to seek godly friendships, even if it isn't in my home group.

"Amen," she said.

Then she bolted from the seat. "Thanks again, Matt."

Before he could reply, she closed the car door with a heavy thud. He waited until she entered her home before he started his car and drove home.

Kelly Sutton was something else. He shook his head. So much pain. She needed friends—a church family to surround her and help her walk through that pain. She needed trustworthy people to come alongside her. More than just Kyle.

As the garage door squealed down the tracks and closed behind his car, Matt wondered if he could be her friend, even if she decided not to join his home group. Not that he had much time to give between work, seminary, and his internship. But, if it was God's Will, He would make the time in Matt's schedule.

After Matt entered his house and sat down at the kitchen bar. He tossed his keys on the counter. Then he punched the power button on his laptop. Might as well get ahead on school work with the rest of his day.

"WHAT'S THE STORY with Kelly?" Matt asked Kyle as they sat down at the kitchen table for dinner. The morning he had spent with her replayed over in his mind ever since he had finished his paper for school.

"How is she?"

"She seemed… Troubled. Sad."

"But the panic attack?" Kyle asked.

"That? She's fine. The EMTs wanted her to go to the hospital, but she refused. I stayed with her for a couple of hours."

Matt chewed thoughtfully on a piece of juicy steak as he waited for a response to his earlier question.

"Thanks for doing that," Kyle said as he ran a hand through his hair. "I think I told you we were friends in college, right?"

"Yeah."

"She had a hard time. The panic attacks started shortly before she started college. Something to do with her dad or her parents' divorce. I don't really remember."

"Did you know her dad was a pastor?"

When Kyle's head jerked back, Matt hoped he hadn't broken a confidence. He let out a slow breath as Kyle nodded his head.

"Now that you mention it, I think she had told me that a long time ago. He was before her parents divorced. Yeah. That's all I know."

Matt scraped a forkful of baked potato out of its shell. He frowned as he savored the sweet bite, trying to figure out the significance of Kelly's confession. He shook his head. Reading into it would take him nowhere helpful.

He steered the conversation away from Kelly and asked Kyle about his plans with his girlfriend Niki for New Year's Eve. Kyle's eyes lit as he explained the romantic dinner he planned. Then the conversation waned as they finished their meal.

Matt stood and gathered the dishes. After he loaded the dishwasher, he entered his bedroom, sucking in air between his teeth. He forgot he had left it a mess in his rush that morning, so he put everything in its place.

Thoughts of Kelly came to mind. Her pretty brown eyes and her sweet smile that appeared once some of her anxiety eased. He was glad he spent the morning with her. And that he introduced her to his long-time friend, Dwight.

Once he finished straightening his room, Matt retrieved his phone and tapped on Kelly's contact info. He typed out a text message. Then he deleted it before he tried again.

Did you talk to Dwight?

A few seconds later, the answer came. *Interview tomorrow. Thanks.*

Anytime.

He didn't expect a response, so when it arrived, he skimmed it.

Thanks for… Listening. Helping.

A smile twitched at the corner of his mouth.

Of course. LMK how the interview goes. Praying for you.

She sent back the thumbs up emoji.

Matt set his phone down and leaned back on his bed, humbled to have played a role in helping Kelly settle in.

5

Kelly

FRIDAY MORNING, KELLY texted Kyle. *Door is open. Come on in.*

Thankfully, he agreed to watch Alana while she went to her interview. The daycare said they were closed for the day, as only a handful of parents signed up for childcare that day. So frustrating. Perhaps once she settled into her new job, she could find more reliable care.

She powdered her face before applying some earth-toned eyeshadow. Just enough to enhance her appearance without looking glam. Years ago, she learned the value of subdued makeup and modest clothing in her role as an event planner. Look professional, but not like the attendees. Too many men hit on her during those first few years.

As she spritzed on setting spray and the cool drops dampened her skin, she heard Kyle's voice downstairs.

"Hello!"

"Daddy!" Alana's squeal faded as she ran down the stairs.

Kelly smiled as her heart warmed. Yeah, that was why she moved. She sighed as she thanked God for bringing her to Arizona.

"Mmmm. Pumpkin, you look so pretty today. What do you want to do first?"

Kelly fastened a simple gold necklace on. Then she secured her classic Timex watch. The only fancy thing about it was the pretty gold band. Then she slipped on a pair of pumps and headed down.

Kyle let out a low whistle as her pumps clicked across the hard tile floor.

"Kel, I can see where Alana gets her good looks."

Kelly laughed at his teasing. She appreciated the compliment, even though she always thought he was easy on the eyes, too.

"When are you gonna put a ring on Niki's finger?" she asked.

He waggled his eyebrows. "That's why I need you to be back by two."

"Gotcha. Sweetie, do you have your backpack?"

"Yes, Mom."

"She's already had breakfast," Kelly said as Kyle held the door open for her and Alana. "So don't let her trick you into an early snack or anything."

Kyle flashed a sheepish smile. "I thought I might treat her to some popcorn at the movie theater. I heard a princess movie is playing."

"I love princesses!" Alana exclaimed.

"I know you do, Pumpkin."

Kelly locked the door before she gave her daughter a kiss on the cheek. "Be good for your daddy."

"We'll be praying for you," Kyle said. "Matt is too."

The mere mention of Matt's name caused her stomach to tie itself up in knots.

"Thanks."

She waved as Kyle held Alana's hand and walked towards his truck. Then she slid into her old car, typed in the address on her phone, and drove over to the resort. As she merged off the freeway, she made her way over to the left lane, which went past the Gila River Casino and Hotel run by the rez.

At the next stoplight, she saw the beautiful stone sign carved with the name of the resort. The navigation on her phone showed the resort and conference center were still a good half mile or more away. She watched for golf carts and quail, as the subdued signs warned. When she glanced to the right, she saw beautiful mountains rising from the desert landscape in the distance. Pinks and tans made them glow in the morning light. The bright green of the golf course completed the picturesque view. She could get used to working in such a serene setting.

The lane wove to the east. Off to her right, she noticed the rust-colored rock sign for the day spa. A matching rust adobe stucco building blended in with the perfectly manicured desert plants.

Slowly, the lane meandered south again, past the conference center. Even though her appointment was at an office by the conference center, she drove the rest of the way to the hotel. She pulled into the guest parking area and studied the place. Maybe heels weren't the smartest choice. It looked like she would be on her feet a lot, just walking between the hotel, restaurant, and conference center.

As Kelly pulled through an empty parking space, she turned back toward the conference center. Once she found an inconspicuous spot for her dumpy vehicle, which looked so out of place compared to the majestic resort, she turned it off. Then she slung her stylish Coach bag over her arm—her work purse, as she called it. The black bag went with everything. Though it set her back a pretty penny, she never regretted owning one fine purse that held everything she needed as she buzzed around the resort.

She quickly spotted the building where she would interview while she strolled toward the conference center. The sound of her heels clicked against the rough pavement. Before she opened the door, a short man with dark hair and a kind smile greeted her.

"Kelly Sutton?"

"Yes."

He held out his hand. "Dwight Durham. Pleasure to meet you. This way."

Dwight held the door open for her. Then he led her down a maze of hallways. The thick carpet swallowed the pointed heel of her pumps. Everything looked new. Fresh wallpaper reminiscent of tall wheat fields coated the walls. The rust and gold tones in the carpet complimented the brass fixtures on the wall. Paintings by native artists with ancestral themes broke up the monotony of the wallpaper. Little cubbies with recessed lighting highlighted intricate native pottery. Clearly, the resort respected and promoted local artists from the rez.

"Here we are," Dwight said at last. "Have a seat. Would you care for some water?"

"No, thank you."

As Dwight sat across from her behind his large dark wood desk, his gold eyes sparkled. She figured he must be in his mid-thirties. Only a few years older than her.

"Matt spoke highly of you. Said you just moved to Arizona so your daughter could be closer to her dad. Admirable, really, picking up and starting over like that."

She laughed. "Admirable or insane. I haven't decided which yet."

"Completely understand. Still, it's good for your daughter to have him in her life. What is her name?"

"Alana."

After she handed him a copy of her resume, Kelly sunk into the soft comfort of the plush leather chair, feeling her nerves slowly melting away. The earthy smell of the leather tickled her nose.

"So you worked for a resort in Colorado Springs for five years?"

Kelly nodded and talked about some of the major events she had managed over the years. Everything from celebrity weddings to huge conferences to smaller private events. After thirty minutes of answering questions, Dwight shared more about the position.

"Our current event planner is leaving us in mid-January.

This week she decided she would not come back after maternity leave. So your timing is perfect."

Dwight tapped his papers on the desk. Then he stood.

"If you're interested, I'd like to offer you the job." He named the starting salary and benefits.

Kelly kept her features slack, despite the unexpectedly high salary. It was more than she made back in Colorado.

She stood and smoothed out her skirt. Then she shook his hand. "I accept. When do I start?"

"If you have time, I'll introduce you to Mita. Then we'll take you on a tour of the property. Can you start on Tuesday?"

Kelly agreed and accepted his offer of a water bottle, imprinted with the resort's logo, which she dropped into her purse.

Mita's office was next to his. When he knocked on the door, a lovely woman with almond-shaped eyes and shiny black hair looked up. Her smile welcomed Kelly as much as her greeting.

After the introductions, Dwight and Mita showed Kelly around the administrative office in the conference center. Then they led her through the hotel lobby. A beautiful hand-painted mural covered the domed ceiling above them, depicting the history of the people who lived on the land long before it became part of the United States. Soft wood wind music filled the open space. A two-story waterfall fountain trickled down, adding a peaceful element to the room which opened up to a bar.

When they turned toward the restaurant, the natural beauty and artistic touches continued. A floor-to-ceiling tile mosaic covered the enormous wall behind the hostess stand.

"The local artist took the better part of the summer to apply all the quarter-inch glass tiles," Mita explained. "Mem-bers of the Gila River tribe handcraft all the artwork at the resort. Many residents, including myself, work here. The resort has partnered well with the local community."

"It's stunning," Kelly reverently whispered. "Do you have information about all the artists?"

"Yes. I'll share the notebook with you so you can memorize the stories. Our guests enjoy hearing about them."

Dwight had another meeting, so he excused himself before Mita introduced Kelly to the head chef and his sous chef. The smell of fresh spices and herbs permeated the noisy kitchen. The introductions were short-lived when a large pot clattered onto the floor and the men hurried toward the sound.

"You'll be working primarily with Chef Trenton Foley or his sous chef, Armando De la Mora, for events. We have two restaurants on the property, as well as a poolside café and the bar. Chef plans the food for everything except the five-star restaurant on the roof. That is only open during winter and a different chef manages it."

Mita introduced her to the concierge and a few other staff members before leading her back to the office. Kelly's stomach growled, so she looked at her watch. One in the afternoon. She needed to head back home to relieve Kyle soon.

When Mita noticed, she told Kelly they would pick up on Tuesday. Kelly thanked her and Dwight before she left.

Once in her car, she kicked off her pumps and dug her flip-flops from the backseat, thankful she had left them there. Her sore toes curled against the soft soles. She would have to invest in more comfortable low heels or flats with all the walking she would be doing.

Just as she pulled into her covered parking spot at home, her phone pinged. As she turned off the car, she retrieved it. Matt.

How did it go?

She smiled as butterflies fluttered in her stomach. *Got the job. Thanks so much!*

As she tossed her phone back into her purse, it chimed again. She ignored it until she opened her door. After she set her purse on the counter, she checked her phone again.

Wanna grab coffee? Tell me more?

Kelly's heartbeat picked up pace. She would enjoy Matt's company.

Have to wait for Kyle to drop off Alana.

Her phone rang, and she answered it.

"It's Matt. Hey, Kyle has Alana over here, if you want to come over. I'll make us coffee and we can talk."

"Alright. I'll be over shortly."

She rushed upstairs to change out of her skirt into jeans and a pair of comfy Uggs, much more excited than she ought to be.

6

Matt

MATT QUICKLY LOADED the dishwasher and wiped down the countertops. After checking the hall bath, he fluffed the throw pillows on the sofa and neatly stacked the car magazines on the coffee table. A glance at the table made him frown. He grabbed some furniture polish to wipe down the smooth wood top.

"What's got into you?" Kyle asked from the open door of his bedroom.

"Just picking up the place." Matt tried to keep his voice light.

Kyle snorted. "Deep cleaning is more like it. You got a woman coming over or something?"

Matt froze as the words cut to the truth. There was nothing wrong with cleaning up a bit. It meant nothing.

"You don't spend this much time cleaning up before home group," Kyle added.

He felt his face grow warm as he nervously cleared his throat, the sound rattling in the silence.

"Kelly is coming over. I just don't want the place to look like a bachelor pad."

"It is." Kyle laughed, and his eyes flashed with mirth. "Besides, Kelly doesn't care."

But I do. The admission concerned Matt. It wasn't like he asked her to come over for a date. It was just coffee.

Coffee!

He pivoted back to the kitchen and turned on the

Keurig. Then he restocked the k-cup holder with a variety of coffee choices. Because he hosted home group every week, he always kept lots of different flavors on hand.

The doorbell rang, and Kyle darted past him to get it. Drat, he thought as he fisted his hands at his side.

"Come on in. Don't mind the cleaning product smell," Kyle joked. "Matt was in a mood."

Matt narrowed his eyes at Kyle's back. Sometimes roommates were a pain.

As Kelly entered the great room, he offered a heart-felt smile. She wore a flowing emerald green blouse with high-waisted jeans that showed off her trim waist. Camel-colored Uggs completed the ensemble. Even dressed casually, she looked gorgeous. He mentally kicked himself for staring too long.

"I hope you don't mind," she said as she held up a sub wrapped in paper. "I picked up some lunch. Didn't have time to eat yet."

Matt berated himself in a soft whisper. He should have asked, knowing her interview had been hours ago. Of course, she was starving.

"I had just arrived home when I received your message."

"You still want coffee?" he asked, suddenly feeling very aware of her gaze. He swiped his sweaty palm down his pant leg.

"Of course."

When she flashed him a heart-stopping smile, his throat went dry.

"Mommy!" Alana launched herself against Kelly's side. She set her sub sandwich on the counter and crouched down to hug her daughter. Her obvious love for her daughter tugged at his heart, making him wonder what it would be like to have a family of his own.

When his face heated, he turned toward the coffeemaker and set out two large mugs. He took a steadying breath before tossing a question over his shoulder.

"Room for cream and sugar? I have a few different fancy creamers, too."

"Yes, please. If you have anything with caramel, that's my favorite."

As he placed a mug under the dispenser, she joined him. He swallowed the lump in his throat that formed because of her nearness.

"Wow. That's a lot of options."

"See any you like?"

As she leaned forward, he caught a whiff of strawberries, which sent his pulse skittering. It had to be her body wash. The thought brought warmth to his face, and he scooted away from her.

"I'll take the Sumatra. It's my favorite."

"Excellent choice. Please have a seat at the table and I'll bring it over."

She thanked him as she unwrapped her sandwich at the table. "Alana, you hungry?"

"No, you don't!" Kyle warned from his room. "She had lunch already."

Kelly gave Alana a conspiratorial look before she handed Alana part of a cookie.

"What Daddy doesn't see won't hurt him."

"I heard that."

Matt smiled at the exchange. It was nice to see the two of them getting along so well. He knew Kyle had been nervous about Kelly moving to town and what a long-term friendship might look like. More than once, Kyle reassured him there was no hint of romance between him and Kelly. Not that it was any of Matt's business. He figured Kyle had been so open about it because they were roommates and in a home group together.

When Kyle entered the great room, Matt barely recognized him. A full tux. If that didn't convince Niki to marry the guy, he didn't know what would. Besides, the two were soulmates. They both knew it. He was happy and a little jealous of his friend.

"How do I look?"

Kyle's uncharacteristic question surprised him. It was the first time he had seen his friend less than confident.

"Like a millionaire," Kelly said. "She knows you're not, right?"

Kyle rolled his eyes as he ran his hands down the lapels of the jacket.

"You look handsome, Daddy."

"Thank you, Pumpkin."

Matt brewed himself a cup of Sumatra as well. Also his favorite. The rich, nutty aroma caused his mouth to water while it brewed. Once it finished, he set one mug and a bottle of caramel creamer in front of Kelly with a spoon. Then he retrieved the second mug and poured a dash of vanilla creamer in it. He stirred it before he joined Kelly at the table.

Kyle took off for his date. Something about running a few errands first.

Alana asked if she could watch one of her shows on her tablet. When Kelly agreed, Matt offered to help her with it.

"Seems like I'm always thanking you," Kelly said as he took a seat at the table again.

Her brown eyes held his gaze for a minute, sending his pulse thrumming. He didn't know what was wrong with him. Two days ago, he hadn't felt this energy zing between them. Matt wasn't sure what to do with that. Only that he liked it.

As Kelly swallowed the last bite of her sandwich, she crumpled up the paper and stood.

"Here, let me take that," he said as he shot to his feet.

Her fingers brushed his, sending sizzling heat along his arm. He snagged the creamer bottle too and hurried into the kitchen to put it away and toss the paper. After a steadying breath, he joined her at the table again, hoping his reaction would subside.

After he asked her about the interview, he listened as she described the resort. He had been there before, but the sound of her voice captivated him as she described it.

"How do you know Dwight?" she asked.

"We were friends in college. After I got saved."

"Oh? So you're a newer Christian?"

Matt laughed. "Only if thirteen years is considered new?"

When Kelly's cheeks colored with pink, he smiled.

"I thought you were younger... Um."

"I graduated from college eleven years ago. Got saved as a sophomore. Joe, our other roommate, had been my roommate in college."

Matt weighed just how much of his past to reveal. He barely knew her and the way she affected him... He didn't want to scare her off.

"Let's just say I was a bit of a bad boy back then."

"I can't even picture it." She appeared sincere, which had his pulse doing funny things again.

"The short version is that Joe led me to Christ and Dwight was our home group leader throughout the rest of college. He helped me learn how to study the Bible."

"Is he the reason you wanted to go to seminary?"

Her features twitched when she said "seminary," causing Matt to hesitate. Something about it sent up warning flares.

"No. That's a much longer story," he said, dodging the question altogether.

Just then, the door from the garage flew open. Joe's laughter preceded him. Tori Callahan hung on his arm until she spotted Matt. Then she quickly dropped her arm to her side. Joe took a grocery bag from her before he placed his hand on the small of her back and guided her further into the great room. Then he headed into the kitchen to empty the bags. Matt wondered if Joe finally worked up the courage to ask her out.

"Hey, Kelly, Matt," Joe greeted them as the laughter faded from his voice, but not his eyes.

Tori looked around the room. "There's my favorite little munchkin!"

Alana jumped to her feet, squealing as she ran toward Tori's open arms.

Kelly greeted Joe before he introduced Tori as a friend.

"Hey, you want to join us on Sunday?" Joe asked.

Matt held back a frown. He planned to ask her before she left and didn't like Joe beating him to it.

"We're having a BBQ after church," Tori said. "Joe bought out half the butcher shop, I think."

Joe grinned. "Gonna fire up the smoker overnight. Stuff it with a brisket and drop some ribs in before church."

Matt studied Kelly. She bit her lip and twisted her fingers, so he hurried to explain.

"We all go to church together. Kyle, Joe, me, Tori, Niki, Marcy, and Chad. They have a children's program for Alana, too."

"I… Maybe."

"We usually meet in the lobby by the coffee shop at ten. Service starts at ten-thirty," Matt said. "If you decide you want to meet us, just text me. I'll keep an eye out for you."

"Even if you don't come to church, you can still come over here at noon," Joe added. "I'll have the smoker loaded with too much food. We'll need help to eat it all."

Kelly snorted. "With three bachelors living here, somehow I doubt that."

Matt felt more at ease as she relaxed. He hoped she would change her mind and join them. Whatever her hang up was, she clearly knew the Word. No one knows Psalm 121 is a Psalm of Ascent without knowing their way around the Bible or growing up in a church. There was definitely a story lurking in Kelly's past. He wanted to help her with whatever it was.

7

Kelly

KELLY'S HANDS TREMBLED as she wrung them together, her anxiety rising as she got ready for church. Kyle texted Friday night that he hadn't proposed to Niki yet, so he picked up Alana for the weekend. At least she didn't have to worry about getting her daughter ready, too.

When her throat constricted, she closed her eyes. She could not have a panic attack. Not before church. It wasn't like anyone knew about her past or her father and what he did. She would be one face in a sea of many. Only acquainted with a few people. Kyle knew the most, and he barely knew anything. Not the worst of it.

She slid down to the floor of her bathroom as the wheezing started. Once she grabbed her phone, she tapped on the first contact and typed out: *Can't breathe. Pray.*

Then she bent over so the blood would flow to her head. Kelly hated the attacks and didn't know why the thought of going to church triggered her today. She used to go every Sunday when she lived in Colorado.

Her breathing normalized right as her phone pinged.

Matt. Her face heated. She forgot he was the first contact now. Not Kyle. She really ought to sort her contacts by first name instead of last.

Want me to stop by? Praying either way.

She typed back a message that she would be fine and she would see him at church.

After she stood, she splashed cold water over her face.

The lyrics from one of her favorite worship songs came to mind. *You're the air that I breathe.* She straightened her back and sucked in a deep breath, letting air fill her lungs from the bottom up. Just because Matt's church was a mega-church didn't mean anyone would learn about her or what her father had done. Besides, that happened over eleven years ago. Old news by now.

Kelly held her head high and squared her shoulders. Then she finished her makeup and fixed her hair before she chose a cute pair of casual sneakers. She grabbed her canvas purse and headed out the door.

You are the air I breathe. As she drove closer to the enormous church, she kept murmuring the words. She recited them out loud as she found a parking spot. She thought it might be next to Kyle's truck or one just like it.

As Kelly exited her car, she felt the warmth of the sun on her skin. She left her sunglasses on to block the bright light. Besides, not letting anyone see her eyes at the moment made her feel safer. Then she strolled toward the lobby. Before she spotted the coffee shop, she heard her name.

"Kelly!"

She closed her eyes for a second to steady her nerves. When she opened them, she took off her sunglasses and smiled at Matt.

"You made it. Plenty of time to spare."

"Yeah. About that text. I'm sorry. I thought I was texting Kyle."

When Matt's eyes lost their twinkle, she wished she could take back her words.

"No worries. I was happy to pray for you."

"Am I the only one here?" she asked.

"The gang is all here. Kyle's checking Alana in for class. Would you like some coffee first?"

"Um… Sure."

Matt placed his hand at the small of her back and tingles traveled up her spine. She had felt nothing like it before. Not with Derek. Or any other boyfriend.

"Caramel Macchiato?" he asked.

A brief flutter danced in her stomach. "You remember-ed."

"Of course." He grinned at her.

Of course. Like her choice of coffee was significant enough to remember.

After he ordered his drink, he ordered hers. And paid for both. His kindness took her aback, and she felt unworthy of it.

"You didn't have to do that."

"I don't think a five-dollar coffee is going to break me."

He winked at her and heat settled over her cheeks.

A few seconds later, his home group friends swarmed her. Tori gave her a hug like they were long-lost friends. Marcy, Kyle's sister and Alana's aunt, hugged her, too. Niki didn't. No surprise there. It would take time for Niki to warm up to her, given her history with Kyle. Kelly understood it. Joe and Marcy's husband, Chad, greeted her with a head bob.

After the group chatted for several minutes, they made their way into the massive sanctuary to the stadium seating. Kelly followed behind Tori while Matt followed her. Some-how, she ended up between the two of them.

When the first strains of music blared, Kelly's uneasiness faded. She recognized the song, so she closed her eyes and sang with gusto. Her heart filled with worship as she released her worries to the One who never slumbered.

The message seemed appropriate for New Year's Day. Looking forward. Resolving to trust God more. Exactly what her move to Arizona represented. The pastor ended with a challenge to make time with God a priority, words that held conviction for her. She hadn't settled into a routine yet.

After the service, Joe hurried home to check on the food. Once they were in the lobby, Kyle told her he would pick up Alana and bring her home. So, Kelly walked to her car.

"Can I trouble you for a ride?" Matt asked as he jogged up next to her. "I rode with Joe this morning."

"Oh, alright."

Kelly donned her sunglasses as he fell into step next to her. When the urge to hold his hand came out of nowhere, she gripped the strap of her purse instead.

"What did you think?" he asked as he slid into the passenger seat.

"Very similar to my church back in Colorado."

"Did you go often?"

"Every Sunday."

Kelly pulled out of the parking spot and waited in the line to exit the lot, feeling a little awkward in the silence.

"You said you work at the church, too?"

"Yeah. I work with the high school kids. Mostly during the mid-week program on Thursday nights and special events. Sometimes I fill-in for the youth pastor on Sunday morning."

"You're a brave man dealing with a bunch of teenagers."

Matt laughed. "Maybe so. They're great. So eager to learn. I wish I'd had something like that when I was their age."

The regret in his voice touched a nerve in Kelly. She had been part of a big youth program at that age and it had been the source of much of her pain and baggage. Especially after her father's very public fall and subsequent resignation. Her so-called friends' reaction made it hard for her to trust people or have meaningful friendships. Ironically, Kyle had been the one person she had opened up to, and not even that much.

She felt Matt's eyes on her as she bit her lip and the stinging started behind her eyes. She wouldn't dissolve into tears. Surely after eleven years, she had gotten past all of that.

Matt rubbed his hands together. "I can't wait to eat. Joe makes the *best* smoked brisket. His ribs are delish too, but brisket is my favorite."

Kelly sighed, grateful for the change of topic. It was uncanny how easily he sensed her moods.

"Should we stop somewhere to pick up anything? I didn't bring a side dish."

"Naw. We have plenty of food. Just enjoy yourself today."

After she turned onto his street, she parked in front of the house. Then she followed Matt in. She stopped short at the sight of a little boy sitting next to Alana at the coffee table.

"Who's that?" she asked.

"Oh, that's Tavell, Joe's nephew."

"Kyle, get the door for Joe," Tori said as she nodded toward the sliding glass door.

Kyle quickly opened it and Joe stepped through with a huge tray of meat. Kelly's stomach growled when the smoky smell hit her as he walked toward the kitchen.

"Smells delicious."

Matt smiled. "It's a wonder Kyle and I haven't gained twenty pounds living with the guy."

"We'll let this rest for a few minutes," Joe said. "Ladies, can you set out the rest of the food?"

"Sure thing," Marcy said before she started pulling containers from the fridge.

Tori carried some food to the kitchen bar. Kelly took a few while Niki dug through a drawer for serving spoons. Kyle pulled a caddy of plastic silverware and disposable plates from the pantry.

Suddenly, the area felt too cramped for Kelly, with eight adults moving around the kitchen and dining area. She headed over to the sofa where Alana and Tavell watched a show on Alana's tablet. The boy's dark eyes went wide at something on the show and he ran a hand over his cornrows. Alana giggled.

"You're funny," she said to her new friend.

Kelly smiled as her mom-heart filled with joy seeing her daughter make a new friend.

"They hit it off well." Matt's deep voice sounded beside her. "Joe thought they might. It's why he was so eager to watch his nephew today while his sister, Sheylinn, is at work."

"I hope she made a few friends at church, too. It's been hard uprooting her. We've had so many changes over the last year. Between Kyle coming into our lives again, Derek leaving, and us moving, I've worried it has been too much."

Kelly glanced over at Matt as she felt his eyes on her again.

"Seems like she's adjusting well."

She snorted. "Better than me, I think."

Matt touched her arm. "Give it time. You'll make some friends too."

She angled toward him. As her gaze roamed over his face, she noticed how handsome he looked with those gorgeous hazel eyes and a soft smile. His sandy brown hair parted to one side. The most attractive thing about him wasn't even his perfect build or height. It was his calm, comforting demeanor. Matt Dixon was a man that cared about people. Even her. Even after a few short days.

Brief pulses raced up her arm from where his hand lingered. If she wasn't careful, she might just fall for him. Romance was the last thing she needed in her life. She had a new job starting in two days. There were still boxes to unpack. A new life to get used to.

No, she had no place for a new man. Didn't she?

8

Matt

MATT SWALLOWED HARD as Kelly's eyes roamed over his face. The more time he spent with her, the more he couldn't tear his eyes from her. She was so beautiful, especially when she allowed her barriers to drop for a few minutes.

"It's ready!" Joe announced, stirring Matt from his thoughts.

He realized his hand still rested on Kelly's arm. Heat inched up his neck and face as he dropped it to his side.

"I'll pray, since Matt seems to be distracted," Chad said before he winked and bowed his head.

Even more heat covered Matt's face as he bowed his head for the blessing.

"Amen," the group echoed.

"Let's dish up for the kids first," Tori suggested. "Tavell, come here and I'll help you."

Joe's nephew jumped to his feet. Alana followed behind, and Kelly quickly caught up to her.

Matt's eyes followed her as she held a plate for her daughter. Her love for Alana seemed so obvious. She was a great mom. He watched as she dished up pulled pork, brisket, and mac n' cheese onto Alana's plate. When her gaze met his, his heart palpitated.

"Do you have any small bowls for the salad?" she asked from across the room.

"Got it," Kyle said as he opened the pantry. He set a stack near the plates.

Matt's voice left him, and his feet rooted to the ground.

"Careful, cowboy," Joe said as he nudged him back to reality.

Matt snorted, as he was about as different from a cowboy as pears were to lemons.

"She just got out of a long-term relationship."

"I know that."

"And she just moved here. The gal has plenty on her plate."

Matt frowned, even though Joe was right.

"So stop gawking at her and get yourself some food."

He held back a groan and stepped forward in line. As he plopped some ribs and brisket on his plate, he tried to figure out why Joe's observations bothered him so much. It wasn't like he hadn't thought the same things. He had. Every time he thought about Kelly, he reminded himself of all the reasons she should be off-limits.

None of it mattered. Not to his heart. He wanted to ask her out.

Only it would be foolish to do so. He just met her. Any other woman he had dated, he had waited significantly longer before even suggesting a first date.

Something was different about Kelly, though. He felt connected to her, unlike any other woman he had met. Even now, without looking her direction, he could tell her eyes followed him.

"Excuse me, Matt," Niki said. "We forgot to put out the lemonade."

He flattened himself against the counter so she could open the fridge to retrieve the pitcher. When she closed it, he grabbed his food and headed to the last seat at the table, directly across from Kelly. He had the best view in the room.

Matt listened to the conversation around the table while he ate. He appreciated that both Marcy and Tori asked Kelly questions, getting to know her. He understood it might take Niki more time to warm up to her, given Kelly's history with

Kyle.

When it looked liked everyone had finished eating, he gathered the empty plates and tossed them in the trash. Then he retrieved a garbage bag to replace the overly full one. As he opened the sliding door, his phone rang.

Mom.

His stomach tightened as he swiped his thumb across the phone to accept the call. Rarely did Mom call just to chat. It was always something.

"Hey," he said as he balanced the phone on his shoulder while he tossed the trash into the bin outside. The lid fell closed with a soft whoosh.

"Hey, Matt. How are you doing?"

"Fine."

"Listen, I need a favor."

And here it comes.

"Actually, it's your brother that needs the favor."

Matt paused on the back porch as needles jabbed his spine. He frowned and asked, even though he didn't want to.

"What's Mark gotten himself into now?"

"Well. Um. They evicted him."

Matt closed his eyes and clenched his jaw, waiting for the inevitable.

"And he's been crashing on our couch for a few days. He needs a place to stay."

He shook his head emphatically, as if his mother could see him. "He can't stay here. Not if he's still—"

"He swears he's clean."

"Mom, swearing it and being it are two different things. He can't stay at my place. Kyle's daughter spends way too much time here. He won't want her exposed to drugs."

"Well, he can't stay with me either," his mom said, as if that explained everything.

"Why not?"

"Greg..."

Matt exhaled loudly. His stepfather was a smart man. Probably didn't want drugs to end up in his home, either.

"Look, I've got a house full of guests. I gotta go."

"So you'll consider it then?"

"Not a chance. Like I said, there's a little girl that lives here a few days a week. The trouble Mark brings isn't something I want to be around, much less—"

"Matt. He's at your front door. You tell him then."

Matt cursed. He hadn't cursed in years, yet a few choice ones flew from his lips as the line went dead.

"Hey," Joe said, sticking his head out the back door. "Your brother is here."

"So I heard. I'll go deal with him."

Matt brushed past his friend and swallowed down bile when he saw his brother. Unshaven. Filthy clothes. The smell of sweat and urine hung in the surrounding air. Hadn't Mom said he had been at her place for a few days? That must have been a lie. He still looked fresh off the streets.

He hurried over to Mark's side before Mark set down his things and ushered him out the front door.

"What are you doing here?" Matt asked, as he noted the glassy haze in his brother's eyes.

"I need a place to stay."

"It ain't here." He folded his arms over his chest as he widened his stance.

"Come on. You wouldn't toss me out on the street."

Matt snorted. "You can't stay here. Kyle moved in a few weeks ago. He's a single dad with a little girl." So he stretched the truth a little. He didn't care to explain the complicated situation to his addict brother.

"At least let me stay in the garage. Something."

Matt shook his head. "Absolutely not. I'll drop you at the shelter downtown."

"But I'm your brother," Mark whined.

That argument used to work on Matt. He forced the old

guilt down. He wouldn't give in anymore. No good ever came from it.

"Stay here. I'll back the car out and you can drop your stuff in it. Then it's off to the shelter."

Mark called him a string of words he wouldn't repeat in front of a sailor as Matt opened the door. He swiped his keys and wallet from his room.

Joe caught his eye.

"I gotta…" Matt's jaw clenched tight.

"No worries. We're just about to start the board games. We'll see you soon."

Matt read the unspoken words of support from Joe's expression before he ducked his head and entered the garage.

As soon as he backed out, Mark tossed his junk in the back seat. Then he hopped in the front. The stench coming from Mark overpowered the confined space. Matt breathed through his mouth to keep his stomach from roiling.

He didn't say another word as he drove his life-sucking, bottom-dwelling brother to the shelter. There was nothing Matt could do to help him because Mark simply didn't want real, lasting help. Only a quick fix for his immediate discomfort.

When he parked in front of the shelter, Mark accused him of abandoning him, just like their father. Years of counseling did little to soften the deep cut Mark's words ripped open in Matt's heart. He was nothing like his father. Not anymore. And leaving Mark at the shelter was the kindest thing he could do for his brother while still protecting himself.

"Get your stuff and go."

Mark yanked open the back door and scooped his stuff onto the sidewalk. His hand shook at his side as he leaned toward the open passenger door.

"You got any cash?"

Matt shook his head. Money was the last thing Mark

needed.

Mark cursed at him again, then slammed the car door shut. As soon as Mark cleared the vehicle, Matt pulled away. He cracked the windows to clear out the lingering odor.

Within two blocks, he pulled over and let the emotion come. He slammed his palm against the steering wheel. His family. He shook his head as the rage coursed through him.

Titus. He needed to recite Titus 2.

"For the grace of God has appeared, bringing salvation for all people, training us to renounce ungodliness and worldly passions, and to live self-controlled, upright, and godly lives in the present age, waiting for our blessed hope."

Matt recited the verses a second time. And a third.

Renounce ungodliness. That's what the counselor told him. Mark's addiction was ungodly. It was the addiction Matt rejected, not his brother. What his brother really needed was the blessed hope Christ offered. Only he wouldn't listen. Never had.

For too many years, Matt had attempted to help Mark in ways that never proved beneficial and had only resulted in damaging Matt. Boundaries were tough. It sickened his stomach to leave Mark at that shelter. But the hard lessons of the past ten years were lessons Matt had learned well. He wouldn't repeat the same mistakes. Especially if his decision resulted in exposing Kelly's daughter to danger. That he would never do willingly.

After he calmed, he turned on his worship music playlist and drove home, hoping to shake off the shame and frustration of dealing with his brother.

When he punched the button for the garage door to close behind him, he hesitated with his hand on the door to the house. The sound of laughter made the hair on his neck stand on end. His soul hurt and he wasn't sure he could be around joyful friends.

He sighed heavily and opened the door, heading straight for the backyard. Thankfully, the temperature remained in the seventies. Matt paced back and forth on the patio, trying to work out the anxiety coiled tightly in his muscles.

Some rotten host he was.

9

Kelly

KELLY NOTICED THE complete change in Matt's demeanor when he returned and headed straight for the backyard. Her eyes followed him as he paced back and forth.

"Let's take a fifteen-minute break," Joe said.

Then he nodded to the guys. As if some hidden message passed between the three men, they joined Matt on the back patio.

Kelly's eyes remained glued to the brooding Matt. Her heart hurt for him. Clearly, dealing with his brother had been painful. A solid reminder that she wasn't the only person in the room with a dark, broken past.

"Let's pray for him," Marcy suggested. Then the four women bowed their heads as Marcy led a sweet prayer for Jesus's peace and healing on Matt's heart.

When the prayer ended, Marcy stood and started cleaning the kitchen. Niki put away the clean dishes from the dishwasher. Marcy and Tori handwashed the items too big to go in it. Niki wiped down the counters while Kelly watched Tavell and Alana.

The somber mood lifted as Joe came back into the house.

"I need to take Tavell home, but when I return, let's get going again."

A few minutes later, Chad came back inside and poured two glasses of iced tea. Then he joined Matt and Kyle outside again.

Kelly accepted a tea from Marcy who distracted her with

questions about how she was settling in.

"Fine. Matt helped me get a job," she said, grateful again for how much he had done for her in a few short days. She wished she could help him right then.

She explained his connection with the hotel manager, and that seemed to satisfy Marcy's curiosity.

Joe returned just as the other men came back inside. Kyle squeezed Matt's shoulder. Chad patted him on the back. Then Matt took a seat across from Kelly.

"Sorry," he whispered. She wasn't sure if he directed it to her or not.

"No worries. If anyone understands family troubles, it's me."

His hazel eyes held her gaze for a few seconds. Then he forced a smile and asked loudly, "What are we playing?"

Kelly's heart pierced over his bravado. Faking it bothered her. Oh, she was as good at it as the next person. But seeing it on such a genuine man, like Matt. Well, it wasn't right.

As they picked up the game, Matt seemed to relax, though he barely looked at her. She knew that feeling, too. Being embarrassed by publicly aired problems. His problems had only been revealed in front of a few trusted friends. Hers had been in the headlines.

Kelly forced herself away from her comparison-based thinking. It wasn't healthy for anyone, and she knew it.

The next hour flew by. At four, Kelly started gathering Alana's things.

"I need to get this one home, do some laundry, and make sure I'm ready for the week ahead," she said.

Kyle stood and retrieved Alana's backpack and other things from her room. As he handed them to Kelly, he suggested they leave a few outfits for Alana at his place. He planned to buy a second set of some necessities to make it easier on all three of them.

"That would be nice. Thanks."

When Kelly took Alana's hand and led her out to the car, Matt followed behind her. She settled Alana in the back seat and then turned her attention to him.

Matt ran a hand through his sandy brown hair. "I'm sorry about all that. Please know, I would never let my brother stay here. Especially not with Alana around."

Kelly held his gaze. "That was never in question."

He puffed his cheeks and blew out a loud breath. "Thanks for understanding."

She placed a hand on his arm and almost withdrew it as tingles spread through her from the touch.

"Are you alright?" she asked.

Matt placed his hand over hers as their eyes met for a few seconds before his gaze flicked away.

"Things with my family are... Complicated. Drama-filled. Hard."

His thumb brushed the back of her hand as he removed it from his arm.

"I appreciate your concern."

As his fingers released her hand, she smiled.

"If you ever want to talk over coffee, I actually know where a coffee shop is now."

His laughter warmed her heart, and she got the sense he would bounce back from the unexpected encounter with his brother.

"I might take you up on that someday."

Then he reached for the driver's door handle and held it open for her.

"Thanks for inviting me to church and for the BBQ. I haven't had such a pleasant day in a very long time."

"I'm glad you enjoyed it. See you Wednesday?"

"I think so," she surprised herself by saying.

He closed her car door for her and she watched as he waved from the porch with a smile on his face.

On Tuesday morning, Alana acted the part of a saint. Kelly appreciated her daughter's good behavior. Her nervousness over her new job brought enough stress of its own. As she pulled into the employee parking at the conference center, she took a minute to enjoy the scenic beauty of the resort.

Her phone chimed, and she dug it out of her work purse.

Good luck. Praying for your first day. You got this.
Matt.

Without thinking, she sent back a heart emoji. Then she regretted it. She didn't want him to get the wrong impression. She sighed as she armed her car and walked toward the conference center. Too bad there wasn't an undo for sending texts.

Mita greeted her as she entered their office.

"A group arrives on Thursday that is staying through Saturday evening. We have already squared away the food, meeting space, and everything else. We just need to be on hand for any emergencies."

Kelly breathed a sigh of relief. It was good to have Mita for a few weeks during the transition.

By midday, Kelly reviewed all the bookings for the next two months. Mita provided detailed checklists of what she completed for each, which also included the remaining tasks.

"Do we have a set menu for events?" Kelly asked.

Mita showed her where to find the information. "We're very accommodating for a fee, but there are some menus that are more popular than others."

Late in the afternoon, Dwight stopped by to see how things were going. He had her complete the paperwork required by Human Resources. Then he agreed to stay out of her way, with the assurance she could stop by his office if she had questions or needed his help.

The last hour of her day, she planned her to-do list for the rest of the week and the next. Then she drove to the daycare center to pick up Alana and headed home.

Her phone pinged as she pulled into her parking space. She turned off the car and read the message from Matt.

Home yet?

Kelly smiled, wondering about the unexpected question.

Just pulled in.

Be over in 10 with dinner.

Matt Dixon had to be the most thoughtful man in the city. Maybe even the state. It sure was nice not to worry about what to fix for dinner after they had crammed her brain full of new information on her first day.

By the time Matt showed up, Kelly changed into yoga pants, a t-shirt, and fuzzy slippers. It felt good.

She held the door open for him as he brought in two bags of food.

"You know, it's just me and Alana, right?" she teased.

"Don't underestimate how hungry I am." He winked at her. "I hope you like spaghetti and meatballs."

"Sounds wonderful. Thank you for this treat. I rarely get a break from cooking."

When he glanced at her, the warmth in his eyes sent electricity up her back. Something about him drew her in and she tried to remind herself of all the reasons she should not fall for him.

"I will confess that I use sauce from a jar," he said as he set it on the counter. "The meatballs are my secret recipe."

"Mmm. Can I help?"

"Nope. Take a seat and tell me about your first day."

Kelly opened the fridge and poured a glass of her favorite white wine. "Care for some?"

Matt frowned for a second before he masked it. "None for me. Thanks anyway."

Alana asked for juice, so Kelly gave her some before she settled in the living room playing a game on her tablet. Kelly sat on a bar stool and watched Matt mix up the meatballs as she sipped her wine.

"I see garlic, onions. Is that parsley?" she asked.

"I mentioned it's a secret recipe."

"Fine. I'll figure it out. I'm good at that."

He laughed. "Tell me about your day."

She did, and before she knew it, he announced dinner was ready.

"You don't mind if we serve from the pans?"

"Please do. Fewer dishes to wash."

Kelly grabbed some pasta bowls and plates for the garlic bread, along with silverware. She set them on the table. Then she offered Matt a beverage. He opted for unsweetened iced tea. She poured herself a little more wine and iced water.

Once the three of them sat around the table, Matt offered a blessing over the meal. When he finished, Kelly thought how wonderful it was to have a friend like Matt. He asked Alana about her day, and those thoughts of friendship rooted deeper. Anticipation spread through her.

Kelly brushed it away. She had only been single again for a few weeks after a heart-wrenching breakup. She shouldn't be thinking about the future. Not yet.

"This is delicious," she said. "I'm positive you put parsley in those meatballs. And oregano, basil, and a touch of Worcestershire sauce."

Matt's handsome hazel eyes rounded. "No way you tasted that."

Kelly shrugged. "I cheated. I saw you put the Worcestershire in there. The rest I tasted."

"Glad you like it. And that I could make your evening a little easier."

As they finished the meal, Matt glanced at his watch. "I should go. I still have to turn in some homework due tomorrow."

"How do you do it all?"

"Late nights, sometimes. I try to stay ahead, but this

week…"

"I didn't ask about you."

"No worries. I'm fine, and tonight was about giving you a break."

Kelly walked beside him to the door. "I really appreciate it."

"Anytime."

Matt's gaze lingered on hers as he made no move to leave. Kelly leaned forward, wondering for a moment if he might kiss her. He cleared his throat and tore his eyes away from her.

"Good night, Kelly."

Yeah, there was definitely something between them. She heard it in the husky timbre of his voice.

"Good night, Matt. Thanks again."

At last, he stepped outside, and she gently closed the door behind him, sighing contentedly. She certainly could get used to spending time with Matt Dixon.

10

Matt

MATT'S HEART RACED as he thought about how close he had come to kissing Kelly. When he looked into her brownish-golden eyes, he felt a jolt of electricity course through his body. Her beauty captivated him.

Once he had become a Christian, he vowed to remain celibate until his wedding night, should he marry. Despite his decision, he was still a man. He could read the signs of Kelly's interest in him. His attraction to her gripped him strongly.

So, there he sat. Trying to prepare for tomorrow night's home group meeting while thoughts of Kelly distracted him. What would it have been like to kiss her? To—

"Hey, how are you doing?" Joe asked from the doorway of Matt's bedroom.

"Fine."

"I've known you too long to know that isn't true."

Matt swiveled his chair to face Joe. "I've got a ton of work tonight. Prep for tomorrow, homework for school, and prep for Thursday."

"Why did you stay over at Kelly's so long?"

Matt's eyes darted to the corner of the room. "I didn't keep track of time after supper."

When Joe leaned against the footboard of his bed, Matt held back a groan.

"Heard from your brother?"

Great. Now he would think about Mark instead of

everything else on his plate. He would much rather think about almost kissing Kelly.

"Nope."

As Matt drummed his fingers on his leg, Joe frowned.

"Something's bugging you. Clearly."

He rolled his eyes. "Could it be that I have a lot to do?"

Joe released a weary sigh and ran his hands down his pants before rising to his feet. "I'm around if you need to talk."

"Thanks, bro."

Joe closed the door when he left.

Matt sighed and ran his fingers through his hair.

Maybe starting with homework first would help. Read God's Word in Greek. That would force him to pay attention.

THE NEXT DAY, Matt crawled out of bed slowly. Taking a peek at his phone, he figured he got about four hours of sleep. He skipped shaving and hurried through his morning routine. Polo shirt and khakis on, he grabbed his work laptop and headed out to his car.

On the way to work, he ordered a mocha, triple shot, and a breakfast sandwich. A quick sip of his coffee gave him a jolt of energy, but it didn't keep him from accidentally deleting one of his formulas in a forecasting spreadsheet. It was after lunch by the time he realized it. When he attempted to get the earlier version back, he failed. So, he spent the next two hours rebuilding it.

Then his boss asked him for a report due by the end of the day. It was rare his boss didn't give him enough time, so he busted it out even though it caused him to leave two hours later than normal.

Even his drive home, usually a fifteen-minute trip, stretched to thirty minutes, and he still hadn't arrived home.

Must have been an accident on the freeway, sending traffic onto the surface streets.

When his phone rang, he glanced at it. Joe.

"Hey."

"Are you gonna make it to home group tonight?"

"I hope so. I'm stuck in traffic." His tires screeched as he slammed the brakes, barely avoiding the car that had almost hit him.

"Kelly brought over a lasagna, so we're sitting down to eat. You want Chad to lead the lesson tonight? He offered."

Matt felt the heavy weight of failure on his shoulders. He was supposed to lead. And be home on time.

"Sure. I don't know how much longer I'll be."

"No worries, bro. We got your back. Kelly set aside some food for you, too."

"Tell her thanks."

"You tell her when you get here."

Matt punched the hands-free button on his steering wheel to hang up the call. His left foot bobbed up and down as he silently urged traffic to move quicker. To soothe himself, he released a few long breaths. His friends could manage without him. Those old voices that damaged his self-respect and self-worth were all lies.

For you did not receive the spirit of slavery to fall back into fear, but you have received the Spirit of adoption as sons, by whom we cry, "Abba! Father!" The Spirit himself bears witness with our spirit that we are children of God.

Years ago, Matt's counselor suggested he memorize several key verses. Romans 8:15-16 were a few of the many he had memorized over the years. He recited them out loud, the sound of his voice competing with blaring horns in the distance.

God saw Matt as a son. A son He wanted and treasured enough to call him adopted. The Spirit's presence in him bore witness to it. *Thank you, Lord, for the reminder.*

Those verses would always hold a special place in his

heart. His earthly father's disdain had left him feeling un-wanted and discarded. His stepfather's dominating behavior was too restrictive, leaving him even more injured and shattered. No wonder Mark ended up drawn to drugs. Matt understood it more than he wanted to admit. His own struggle with alcohol in his early twenties came from the hole in his heart where a father's love belonged.

On days like this, he fought the urge to surrender to the weight of his abandonment, and all the pain that came with it.

But for the grace of Jesus and His Spirit.

At last, he turned onto his street. He pulled into the garage and the sound of the car's engine reverberated in the space as he turned it off. One more calming breath. Then he entered his house.

Chad sat in Matt's usual spot so he could see the entire group. He nodded to Matt and continued leading. Matt realized he should have called Chad yesterday and asked him to cover instead of losing sleep over it last night. Next time, he would do that.

Matt popped into his room and dropped his things on his desk. Then he returned to the great room. Kelly heated his plate of lasagna in the microwave while he poured a glass of iced tea. As he settled into his seat at the table, the smell of melted cheese, herbs, and tomato sauce made his mouth water. When Kelly set the warmed food in front of him, she squeezed his shoulder and offered a sympathetic smile.

Kindness begets kindness.

He mouthed the words "thank you," before he dug in and silently asked God's blessing for the tasty food.

"The video talked about being adopted as sons. Sharing in Christ's inheritance," Chad said.

Matt snorted. He forgot that part. A different verse than the one he recited in the car, but still rejuvenating for his soul.

"Is it hard to believe it? What does that mean to you?" Chad asked the group.

Joe cleared his throat. "Adoption is something close to my heart. My parents adopted my older sisters. Tylissa and Sheylinn were blood sisters. Doctors had told my parents they couldn't have children, so when a friend at an adoption agency told them about two girls they were trying to keep together, my parents jumped on it. Then I was born eight months later."

The group collectively gasped.

"Yeah, I was the surprise, miracle baby. That didn't stop my parents from loving my sisters like their own. Girls that had no future became family, with all the benefits of that word. Family. Children."

"So, when God calls us sons. Adopted as co-heirs with Christ…" Joe shook his head. "Nothing I could ever do gives me the right to be called a son of God. Only Christ's blood made that possible."

Matt let the words penetrate his heart. Then a pressing feeling loosened his tongue. He knew where it came from. The Spirit.

So, he pulled his chair closer to the group and told them the story about his father. The abandonment. The abuse. And what he did with that pain—became an alcoholic until Christ changed him from the inside out, all because his roommate, Joe, had the courage to speak into his life.

No matter how hard it was to be transparent and vulnerable, he never once regretted it. Tonight would be no different.

11

Kelly

KELLY SUCKED IN a sharp breath and rested her fingers near her heart as she listened to Matt's story. Everyone in the room stilled as they listened.

"My father was an alcoholic. When he drank, he brutally beat my mother. And me because I tried to protect Mom and Mark."

A shadow fell over Matt's face. Her heart ached for him.

"Anyway, sometime around when I turned eleven, he took off. Not sure how or exactly when Mom divorced him. Neither Mark nor me saw him again."

He cleared his throat. His gaze darted away from the group.

"Between God sending this guy," he hooked a thumb toward Joe, "and Dwight, I learned about Jesus. Dwight suggested I go to counseling when he learned about my story. One of the smarter things I've done with my life. It was through counseling that I first learned about the notion that God adopted me…"

Kelly felt the moisture on her cheeks as she watched his eyes redden, her throat constricting.

"As a son. A son He wanted. A son He loved."

Matt's lips twisted into a sardonic smile. "The verses from Romans about this are ones I recited on the way home today. Even after all this time, I still need that reminder."

Joe reached over and squeezed Matt's shoulder. Kelly dabbed away the tears that dampened the corners of her eyes.

"Kelly, what about you? How do these verses land?" Chad asked.

She furrowed her brow and scrunched her nose in displeasure. The verses landed horribly. Hard to swallow. She had a loving father whose lies destroyed her trust in just about everyone, even God.

"I'm not ready to share that."

Matt spoke up, his voice a balm against the tension in the air. "It's alright. We don't normally call on people."

Good.

Chad offered a duly chastised smile and moved on.

Too bad Kelly couldn't. The idea of being adopted as a daughter of God, a co-heir with Christ, had once refreshed and quieted her soul.

That was *before*. Before her father's lies. Before his very public ousting that cost her friends, destroyed her sense of well-being and self-worth, and made her question if she could trust ordinary people, much less spiritual leaders.

She had spent the better part of the last eleven years keeping others at arm's length. No one got past her defenses. She would rely on no one. Trust no one.

Until Kyle showed up in her life again. Much of the last year, she had slowly let her guard down. Trusting him little by little with Alana. Trusting him enough to move to Arizona. Believing he really wanted to remain in Alana's life.

But that was different. He was her daughter's father and a good one. She ought to allow Alana the opportunity to know her dad.

Kelly felt the hot tears stinging her eyes before jumping to her feet. Without a word, she darted to the bathroom, hoping she could hide her broken heart a little longer. Thankfully, it had an exhaust fan. The rickety sound muffled her sobs.

A few minutes later, a gentle knock sounded at the door.

"You want to talk about it?" Tori asked from the other side of the door.

Kelly splashed some water on her face. Then she flushed the toilet, too embarrassed to admit she was in there to hide, before she opened the door with a fake smile pasted on her face.

"Sorry. It's free now."

Tori stepped back and shook her head as Kelly pushed past her. Then Kelly squared her shoulders and pasted on her best fake smile as she entered the great room. She sank into the couch, feeling the comforting give of the soft cushion, in stark contrast to the hardness of her heart.

As soon as Chad closed in prayer, Matt joined her.

"Just wanted to let you know you don't have to rush off. We usually hang out and socialize for about a half hour after."

"Oh, okay." Her throat tightened as she glanced at her watch. Seven. Drat. She couldn't even claim needing to get Alana to bed.

"Thanks for bringing food tonight. It was a pleasant surprise and, as you saw, helped me tremendously."

When her eyes met his trustworthy gaze, she nearly spilled her entire story. How he appeared so sincere, she found difficult to believe. She cleared her throat and explained why she brought the meal.

"I got off work early, since I have to work Saturday evening. Thankfully, Kyle has Alana all weekend."

Matt smiled. "Are you working Friday evening too?"

"No. The meeting attendees reserved a private room at the restaurant instead of the banquet room. So I'm off."

Matt rubbed a hand on the back of his neck as he shifted from foot to foot. "I was thinking, if you're interested... I mean... Would you like to go out? Or I could cook for you again?"

Kelly's heart fluttered as her pulse quickened, and her anxiety lessened. "On Friday? We could go out. That sounds nice."

His eyes twinkled as a wide, toothy grin spread across his face. "I'll pick you up at six? Or is that too early?"

"Six-thirty?"

"Great. And Kelly?"

"Huh?"

"I'm really glad you came tonight. And that you stood your ground. Even though this is a safe place, Chad shouldn't have called you out. You were right to stand up to him."

A weight lightened from her shoulders with his words. She wouldn't let anyone pressure her into sharing when she wasn't ready.

BY FRIDAY, KELLY settled into her new job. She appreciated the staff at the resort, especially Mita. Even though Mita would leave in a few days, she hoped they might continue their fledgling friendship.

As she pulled into her parking space at home, she noticed Kyle and Alana walking to his truck. She liked he had a key and could pick up things for their daughter without her being home.

"Alana!"

"Mom!"

When her daughter launched into her arms, she felt her warmth and breathed in her sweet scent. Oh, how she loved her little girl.

"I'm glad we saw you. I always miss you when I'm at Dad's."

Kelly's nose twitched as she fought to contain her emotion. "Thank you, sweetie. I miss you too. Have fun, okay?"

"Love you."

Then Alana turned toward her dad, who held the truck

door open for her.

"See you Sunday!" Kyle called before he hopped into his truck.

Kelly glanced at her watch. Not much time to get ready before Matt picked her up. She better hurry.

Once inside, she dropped her purse and keys on the counter. Then she dashed up the stairs to her room. She changed out of her work clothes and stood before her closet, furrowing her brow.

What to wear?

Her fingers skimmed over several dresses as she considered her options. A sweater dress would be too hot. She really needed to trim down her cold weather wardrobe. When her hand brushed over her favorite black dress, she pulled it from the closet. She liked how she looked in it. Feminine, but not too alluring. Hopefully, it wasn't too dressy for whatever restaurant Matt had in mind.

Just as she finished powdering her face and applying berry-colored lipstick, the doorbell rang. Kelly grabbed a pair of pumps and ran down the stairs. She paused at the door as she put them on. Squaring her shoulders, she opened the door.

Oh, my!

Her smile faltered as her eyes roamed over Matt's appearance. He wore a bright blue shirt, sleeves rolled up to his elbows, exuding a strong manliness. His gold watch sparkled nearly as much as his mesmerizing eyes. She breathed sharply in through her nose, savoring the spicy smell of his cologne. Brand name jeans hugged his legs. Oh, she should stop staring and let him in.

"You look beautiful," Matt said as he leaned forward and kissed her cheek, his lips warm against her skin.

As Kelly moved aside, she could feel the heat radiating from her face.

"You look pretty good yourself." She laughed nervously as she tucked her hair behind her ear. Then she grabbed her purse and keys from the kitchen.

"I debated about flowers… I wasn't sure if you had allergies or anything."

"I don't. Have allergies, that is. At least not to flowers. Grass, on the other hand…"

He jammed his hands into his jeans pockets. "I'll remember that next time I think about gathering a bouquet of grass for you."

Kelly tossed her head back with a laugh. "I can almost picture you following a landscaper around."

He chuckled. Then he nodded toward the door. "Shall we go?"

Once they were in the car, Kelly asked where they were going.

"It's a local steakhouse. Great date place not too far from here."

Kelly leaned back against the seat and sighed contentedly, letting the last remnants of nervousness fade away.

"I can't tell you how nice it is to go out on a Friday night. I can't even remember the last time."

"Oh, so I could have taken you to Texas Roadhouse?"

She chuckled. "Even McDonald's would have been exciting."

He snorted. "I wouldn't do that to you. I'm sure Alana eats plenty of chicken nuggets from there."

"True."

When he reached over and twined his fingers with hers, she enjoyed the way they fit together so perfectly. With his touch, a wave of warmth spread from her fingertips up to her heart.

Her phone rang, and she reluctantly released his hand. She answered it on the third ring. Mom. Suddenly, she felt guilty for no reason.

"Hey Mom."

"Kelly. How's the new job?"

"Good. Is everything okay?"

Her mom hesitated. "Sure. Why do you ask?"

"Can I call you back later? I'm kinda on a date."

"Oh! Um… I need to let you know… Well, never mind that right now. Call me later or tomorrow. It's important, but I don't want to ruin your date, honey."

Ruin her date?

"You're not dying or anything, right?"

"Oh, no, honey. Nothing like that. Have fun!"

The line went silent and Kelly's throat tightened as she wondered what her Mom could say that would upset her.

"Everything okay?"

She took a deep breath. "I think so."

Then she resolved to forget about it until tomorrow. If Mom thought it could wait, Kelly wouldn't think about it. She was out with Matt. Their first date. She wouldn't let her worry wreck her date.

12

Matt

As MATT DRESSED for his date with Kelly, Joe hovered in the doorway.

"Guess you don't mind being the rebound man, huh?"

Matt narrowed his eyes. "She's a grown woman. She can make her own decisions."

"It's too soon. She's only been out of a relationship for what, a few weeks?"

"Layoff, Joe," Kyle said from behind him. "Her engagement had been over long before she received the text from her ex."

"I just don't think it's wise," Joe retorted.

Matt reached for his keys, the jangling mimicking his annoyance as he pushed past Joe. "It's none of your business."

When Joe grabbed his arm, Matt's shoulders tensed.

"You should get to know her more."

Matt jerked free from his best friend's grip. "What do you think the purpose of dating is?"

He didn't wait for a response as he stalked toward to the garage. After he pulled out and drove toward Kelly's place, he tried to shake off his frustration. Sometimes Joe took the whole accountability partner thing too far. It was only a date. One meal. It's not like he was going to stay the night or anything crazy like that. He had principles with no plan to compromise them.

While he waited for Kelly to answer the door, he stretched his neck from side to side.

The second she opened the door, his gaze traveled the length of her and he forgot all about his earlier argument with Joe. She looked gorgeous in her fitted black dress, the luxurious fabric enhancing her shape. And her lips. He swallowed as he wondered what it would be like to feel those berry-colored lips brush across his.

During their conversation on the ride to the restaurant, he settled his spiraling thoughts.

At last, he pulled into the parking lot at Chop Steakhouse, a favorite of his. He had learned about the place from a coworker. After asking Kelly out, he made a reservation for them. Good thing too, judging by the line out the door.

As Matt circled the car, holding the door open for Kelly, the scent of her perfume captivated him. She smiled and whispered her gratitude as she walked past him. Once inside the restaurant, he gave his name, and the hostess quickly seated them in a secluded booth. Perfect. He could not have asked for a better table, away from the clattering of cutlery and hum of conversation.

The hostess handed them menus and a wine list. Kelly reached for it before she quickly withdrew her hand.

"If you want a glass or two, that's fine. Just because I don't drink doesn't mean you can't."

"Are... Are you sure?"

Hoping to put her at ease, he flashed her a sincere smile. "Absolutely. I think it was Sauvignon Blanc?"

Her cheeks reddened. "I didn't think you'd noticed."

He noticed everything about her. Not just her choice of coffee or wine. Those big brown eyes with gold flecks. Her plump, enticing lips. That lipstick.

Matt cleared his throat and forced his eyes back to hers.

"Please, I promise I won't rip it out of your hand and guzzle it or anything."

"It's just..."

Now she had his attention.

"It's just what?"

"My father drilled it into my head as a girl. Christians shouldn't drink around others that…"

Matt reached over and took her hand in his. "Since I'm the one with the past, and I know what I can and can't handle, why don't you trust me? If you want a glass, order it."

When the server arrived, Kelly asked for a glass of wine and an iced tea. Good. One little battle won. He didn't want her to change who she was or what she liked because of him. No woman ought to.

"These prices…" she muttered under her breath, but he noticed.

"Kelly, if I couldn't afford it, I wouldn't have brought you here. It's a nice place with the price tag to go with it. Not a problem. You deserve a little special treatment after the past few months, don't you?"

She tucked her lower lip under her teeth, which sent his thoughts spinning again.

"Order what you want, not what you think I can afford."

When the server came back to their table, she ordered a pricey steak and added on a salad. His mood brightened as he ordered his meal.

"When is the last time you were on a date?" she asked.

He looked up, trying to remember. "It's been years."

Kelly's head jerked back as her eyes widened. "Years? A handsome man like you?"

"It hasn't been a priority," he confessed. "Since I started back to school, I don't have time."

"But you're here. Tonight."

True. Matt figured the right person made all the difference.

"Maybe because I see the end in sight of school. Just a few more months and I'll be done."

"What will you do then?"

He weighed her question as the server brought out the salads, the smell of herbs and vinegar mingling in the air.

"I'm not sure. I originally pursued the degree, intending to become a pastor in the youth program at church."

"What changed?"

You. He couldn't say that on a first date. Nor would he admit that her initial reaction and her hints about her father's former career had him reconsidering how much he wanted it.

"I want to honor God, but I'm not sure if He is calling me to full-time ministry or not. I had hoped it would become clear before I finished school."

"Oh, so you've had doubts from the beginning?"

"Eh. Kinda. I know I'm supposed to work with the high school kids. And I figured going to school would help me learn a lot more about the Bible and God. I just don't know about full-time ministry."

She scrunched her nose. "It doesn't pay well."

He chuckled. "No, it doesn't. But I paid off my house—"

"Wait, you *own* that house?"

Matt nodded and his chest rose, pleased that it surprised her. He had worked hard to save up a huge down payment. Then he sunk every spare penny into it.

"I didn't want to rent. It's four bedrooms. Plenty big enough for my future wi—" He almost said wife and kids. Saying the words to her felt too real, especially when staring into her eyes. "Family. For now, Kyle and Joe rent their rooms, which covered the expense of school."

"So you have *no* debt and own a house?"

"Yup."

She snorted. "Did you win the lottery?"

He shook his head.

"Are you twenty years older than you look?"

He laughed. "Thirty-three. For a few more months."

"Well, I will order two desserts, then. They will let me take them home, right?"

"You can order as many desserts as you want."

The server cleared away the salad plates and set out their meals. He took a bite of the juicy steak and relished the burst of flavor in his mouth. So good.

Throughout the rest of the meal, he asked her about her new job, her favorite foods, and just a bunch of silly stuff. She asked him the same. When it came time for dessert, she ordered two and he ordered one. All to go. She suggested they could eat it back at her house.

After he paid for the meal, it only took a few minutes to get back to her place. Matt suddenly felt a surge of nervous energy coursing through him. He wanted to kiss her. No doubt. Just figuring out the timing. The mood.

He mentally kicked himself. It was their first date. Maybe he should wait. If the kiss turned out to be as amazing as he imagined, it might be wise to go slower.

Like normal, he held the car door open for her once they arrived at her home. Then he carried the food as she led the way inside.

"Where do you want this?"

"Hmm?"

Kelly lowered her lids, her lashes fanning over her cheeks. Then she glanced up at him. Rational thoughts fled his mind as his pulse raced.

"I want a bite of that chocolate dessert," she said as she captured her lower lip between her teeth.

"Just a bite?" he teased.

"Yeah. Otherwise I might explode."

He willed his heartbeat to slow down while he opened each of the containers until he found the chocolate cake and his peach cobbler. He put the rest of the items in the fridge.

Right as he stepped away from the fridge, Kelly reached for the silverware drawer behind him. Her hand brushed his side, sending lightning through his veins. She stopped inches from his body. Between the unexpected touch, her strawberry fragrance, and that berry-colored lipstick, he was a goner.

He wrapped his arms around her as she slid her hands up his chest until they rested behind his neck, sending his pulse screaming. Their eyes met. The world around them faded away as his lips crashed over hers. Her lips were like a gentle breeze, soft and warm against his mouth. He embraced her tightly, his hands exploring her back. Then she parted her lips, and he groaned. She tasted sweet, like she had already snuck a bite of the chocolate dessert. His hand lodged in her silky hair as he deepened the kiss. She leaned into him as she ran her hands over the contours of his back.

Common sense warned him to end the kiss and create some distance. Except the counter blocked him on one side and Kelly on the other. He didn't want the exhilarating kiss to end. It was so much better than he had dreamed.

When Kelly took a step back, she clasped his hand. Her touch sparked through him, skyrocketing his desire. He really should stop. Move away. Go home. Only he couldn't muster the willpower.

13

Kelly

KELLY MELTED INTO Matt as the intensity of the kiss grew. She loved the feel of his hands on her back as his lips tasted hers. Her response surprised her. She wanted the kiss to last longer. Much longer.

Slowly, she backed up, pulling him along with her. The kiss heated as she led him to the couch. Their lips broke apart only long enough for her to recline back. Matt followed her down on the couch.

His lips gently trailed away from hers and left lingering velvety kisses on her neck. She moaned and brought his mouth back to hers, kissing him fervently. Her hands found their way underneath his shirt to his warm skin. His hands roamed over the top of her dress. Still, she didn't ask him to stop. Didn't want to stop.

Her phone buzzed, and she froze. Matt didn't slow down one bit.

But it was her phone. It might be something about her daughter.

Kelly placed a hand on his chest and pushed. "Matt."

His soft lips slowed on her neck.

"My phone."

Then he stopped, both of them panting heavily.

"Where is it?"

"My purse."

As Matt stood from the couch, she felt a wave of heat, followed by a sudden chill. When he held out his hand for her, he pulled her to her feet, then released her as if she might burn him.

"Sorry. It might be Alana."

She hurried over to her purse and snagged her phone.

Love you, Mom. Night.

Kelly sighed and typed back a heart-felt message to her daughter. Then she turned to face Matt.

His stormy gaze reignited everything she had felt a few minutes ago. She wanted to throw herself into his arms again, ignoring all her convictions.

Instead, she circled the corner of the kitchen island and retrieved two forks. She carried the sweet-smelling desserts toward the table.

"It was her. She just wanted to say good night," she said as she placed a fork next to his dessert.

Matt rubbed a hand on the back of his neck, and red flushed his cheeks.

"Sorry I… Got a little carried away."

"It's fine. I'm fine. We're fine."

She picked at the dessert and quickly shoved a bite in her mouth before she changed her mind and leaped into his arms again.

"You want something to drink?" he asked.

"No thanks. Help yourself," she said around the bite in her mouth.

After he poured an iced tea, he chugged half of it, refilled it and joined her at the table. Once he sat down and picked up his fork, Kelly tried to lighten the mood.

"Needless to say, you're a good kisser," she quipped.

His eyes widened as a cough rumbled in his chest. He pounded it a few times before he swallowed the bite. Then he snorted. "You're okay at it."

Then he winked at her and gobbled another bite of his dessert.

"This is good."

She savored the decadent chocolate flavor as the moist

cake melted in her mouth.

"Wanna a bite?"

His hazel eyes latched on to hers. "Tempting, but no."

When she finished, she slid the to-go container away from her. Matt ate his last bite. Then he grabbed the empty containers and forks.

"Allow me to do dishes," he teased. "Before I go."

Her shoulders drooped as her heart yearned to spend more time with him. But he was right. After those electrifying kisses, he ought to leave.

He threw away the containers and placed the forks in the sink before he walked toward her.

"Don't get up. I think we covered the goodnight kiss and then some."

He leaned down and pecked her cheek before he backed away.

"Good night, Kelly."

"Matt?"

He paused, hand on the door.

"Thank you for a wonderful evening. All of it."

He nodded and darted out the door. Not until she heard his car start did she stand and lock the door. Then she leaned back against it.

Some kiss. Wow!

14

Matt

MATT TOSSED HIS keys on his desk with a clank and ran a shaky hand through his hair, still unnerved by his lack of self-control. It had been a long time since he had kissed a woman.

That hadn't been the reason he lost it, though. He liked Kelly. A lot. Clearly, she liked him, too.

Liked or lusted?

The question rocked him to the core, causing his breath to lodge in his throat. Had his feelings been purely physical attraction?

He shook his head as he paced back and forth across the length of his room. No. He *did* care for Kelly. Things like the way she showed concern for him the day his brother showed up. She had cried when he shared the story about his father. That touched him deeply. They shared an emotional connection. Perhaps even a spiritual one. So, he shouldn't judge himself too harshly for wanting a physical connection.

Still, he needed to be more careful. Joe was right. She had just come out of a long-term relationship. Matt should take things slower with her to avoid being her rebound. His heart couldn't take it.

After he sat down at his desk, he punched the power button on his laptop. His mind wandered back to when Kelly opened the door and greeted him. She had taken his breath away as she studied him. Their connection at dinner had been powerful, too. She smiled often. Boy, did he love her smile. And her heart. And the way she cared for her daughter. Kelly Sutton was a wonderful mom, and she would make a wonderful wife.

Matt launched to his feet, his heart slamming against his ribcage. Too soon. Way too soon for that thought.

He walked out to the kitchen and poured himself an iced tea.

When Kyle entered, he asked, "How did it go?"

Matt downed a swig of his drink.

"Great." Amazing enough for his mind to leap towards a long-term relationship.

Kyle smiled. "I'm glad. I think you're exactly the kind of man she needs."

Matt nearly stopped breathing. "You think so?"

"Yeah. And she might just be the kind of woman you need."

Need? He never considered he might need a woman. Or what she might be like. He had been so busy with work, church, and school that it never crossed his mind.

"Don't look so shocked. It's perfectly natural for a man to need a woman. Remember Genesis? God made Eve as a helpmate..."

"Guess that means Adam needed a helpmate, huh?"

"Exactly!"

"You're not just saying that because you're getting married soon?"

Kyle grinned. "Nope. It's okay for you to think about settling down. Finding a woman you want to spend the rest of your life with."

"Why do you think Joe is so against it?"

Kyle snorted. "He can't admit his feelings for Tori. And he's afraid of losing his best friend."

Matt slowly nodded as he saw the truth in Kyle's words.

"When did you get so wise?"

"You know my story. Losing everything important to you changes a man's perspective. Life is short, bro. Happiness is fleeting. *Carpe diem.*"

Kyle opened the dishwasher and set a glass inside. Then he closed it.

"Anyway, glad you had a 'great' time. Night."

Matt tossed a farewell over his shoulder as he walked into his room. Seize the day. Not unwelcome advice.

Though falling in love, choosing a wife, those things would require him to deal with his fears that he could turn into a monster like his father had been. He wasn't sure he was ready.

Trying to clear his mind, Matt opened his paper for seminary and reread it before finishing it up. With the assignment completed, he uploaded it and powered off his computer.

Seminary. Why had he started down that path again? Had he felt called to become a pastor? Was he even cut out for it?

Maybe he should talk to Pastor Chris, the high school pastor. Or maybe even Pastor Miles, the senior pastor. It had been a few months since he met with them about his progress in the internship. Perhaps they saw something in him he couldn't see.

He glanced at his watch. Eleven. Much too late to text either pastor. Besides, tomorrow was Saturday. They would have the morning off and lead services in the afternoon.

Instead, he changed and climbed into bed, feeling more uncertain than he had felt in years. Tomorrow was a new day. Hopefully, clarity would come soon.

15

Kelly

KELLY AWOKE LATE the next morning, groggy from a night of restless sleep. She had relived those kisses with Matt. Clearly, they shared a powerful attraction. But was there something more?

When she thought about Matt, she considered how much he helped her the first day they met. He had called off work to help the friend of a friend—a stranger to him. Who did that?

A man who exhibited the love of Christ.

Her cheeks warmed. She stared up at the ceiling as images of him right before that kiss came to mind. Nothing Christ-like in his smoldering eyes then.

Was that so bad, though? Shouldn't relationships have some level of passion? Passion balanced with self-control. Emotional connection balanced with physical.

Kelly wished she could talk to her mom about stuff like this. Only the relationship between her parents had been a poor role model. Incredibly ironic, given that her dad had been a pastor.

She thought back to the early signs of trouble in her parents' marriage. Dad missed dinner for a meeting one night. Then two. Then it became a regular occurrence. Raised voices at night when he finally came home. Mom's tears when she found lipstick on Dad's collar.

Kelly shouldn't have witnessed the demise of their marriage. But she had had a front-row seat. Dad accused

Mom of being closed off. Unaffectionate. Surly. Mom accused Dad of falling out of love with her. Not caring about her feelings. Then the accusations came about his affair.

A tear rolled down her cheek and neck, the soft pillowcase soaking it up. How could their marital problems affect her so much? Was she like them?

Derek had accused her of being emotionally closed off. Unaffectionate. Like her mother. Though he didn't know that, his words cut deep.

Yet last night with Matt had been the complete opposite. She had opened up with him more in one week than she had with Derek in a year. Those kisses with Matt had been affectionate and passionate.

Maybe too passionate.

Was she like her father? Seeking solace for her wounded heart in the arms of someone else?

The thought caused her stomach to churn. She had no intention of being like him. Ever. She would never be unfaithful to the man she loved. She would never destroy Alana's life, like Dad had hers. Alana came first. Always.

Was that even Biblical? Sure, Alana should be important. But if Kelly ever married, her husband ought to come before her daughter.

Either way, Dad got it all wrong. So very wrong.

Just then, she remembered her mom had called her last night. She should call her back.

Slowly, Kelly rose from her bed. She stuffed her feet into fuzzy slippers and wrapped a soft robe around her. Then she padded downstairs and started some coffee. Once it finished brewing, she tapped on her mom's contact in her phone and called her.

"Morning, honey. How was the date?"

Kelly's cheeks flamed. Thank goodness it wasn't a video call.

"Good."

"Just good?"

"Okay, it was great. Wonderful."

"I'm so happy for you, honey. You're long overdue for some joy in your life."

Wasn't that the truth?

"You said you had something important to tell me?"

Kelly waited while silence answered. She checked to make sure the call hadn't dropped.

"I heard from your father."

Kelly sat up straighter in her chair and frowned as her pulse raced.

"What does Phil think of that?"

"Oh, it's not like that. He knows, of course. But your father asked about you. Said he's gonna be in Arizona soon and wanted to look you up."

Kelly gritted her teeth as sweat chilled the back of her neck. "You told him I was in Arizona?"

"No. He already seemed to know that. He just wanted your address and phone number."

"Mom. Please tell me you didn't."

"He's your father. Haven't you punished him long enough? Don't you think it's time to forgive him?"

"Never. I'll never forgive him."

"Kelly Ann Sutton. You know what the Word says about that. Seventy times seven."

She let out a loud sigh, wearying of the lecture. Even though Mom was right and Kelly knew she ought to forgive her father, she wasn't ready. No amount of Bible-thumping from Mom would change that.

"I'm twenty-nine, Mom. A single mother. I don't need a lecture from you about forgiveness."

"I just think your lack of it is holding you back. I think it's what kept you distant from Derek. Why he cheated on you..."

Her blood boiled at the accusation. "Well, I didn't ask your opinion, did I?" Kelly groused, then immediately felt bad about it.

"Sorry, honey. I don't mean to stir up trouble with you. I love you. And I just thought you would want to know that your father might show up some day soon. It's better to prepare yourself than to be caught by surprise."

That was the first sensible thing Mom said.

"I appreciate it. And Mom?"

"Yes, honey?"

Kelly's shoulders hung low. "Sorry, I snapped at you. I love you too. I gotta get ready for work. There's a big banquet event tonight at the resort."

"Okay. Is Alana around?"

"No. She's with Kyle for the weekend. You can call his number, though. I'm sure she would love to hear from grammy."

"Love you, honey."

The line went dead. Kelly slid her coffee mug further away and dropped her head to the table.

"Ow." Little too hard.

Her dad had her number. Her address. And he would be in Arizona soon.

Her appetite vanished.

She felt her chest constrict, and the wheezing started. Lightheaded. She should have expected the stress. Conversations about her father had always been a major trigger. *Please God, no.*

Sliding down to the cold floor, she slumped over her knees, her vision blurring. One breath. Two.

Then she reached for her phone and typed out a text to Matt. *Please come. Panic attack.*

16

Matt

MATT GLANCED AT his smart watch when it vibrated. He blinked at the words from Kelly. She needed him.

Need.

A cold sweat broke out across his forehead as fear clutched at his heart. He had to go now.

Though he hated to do so, he left the full shopping cart at Home Depot and walked out the door. Then he jogged to his car and called Kyle.

"Pick up, bro," he growled, as his heart slammed against his chest.

"Hey, it's Kyle. Leave a message."

Should he go straight to Kelly? What if she didn't unlock the door? Going home to get Kyle's key would take too long.

Pray.

Lord, please help Kelly. Calm her. Help her settle enough to let me in. Give me the words to help.

His phone rang.

"You called?" Kyle's voice came across his car speakers, his daughter's giggles sounded in the background.

"Kelly's having a panic attack. I'm on the way now, but I'm not sure she'll be able to open the door. Do I call 911? Can you meet me there and let me in?"

"Calm down, bro. No can do. Niki, Alana, and I drove up north for the day so Alana can play in the snow."

Matt slammed his palm against the steering wheel. Stinging radiated through his bones.

"Not to worry. There's an extra key under the planter on the porch. Use it."

"Okay. 911?"

"Probably not. She chewed me out pretty good last time."

"Thanks, bro."

Matt parked in Kelly's community. As soon as the engine shut off, he ran to her home. He spotted the planter he had never noticed before, even after walking past it a dozen times, and retrieved the key. Once he unlocked the door, he rushed to Kelly's side.

"Matt?" Her body muffled her voice as she bent over her legs.

"I'm here, Kel."

He kneeled next to her and gently massaged her back in soothing circles, trying to swallow down his fear.

"Thank. You."

"What do you need? How can I help?"

Her hand reached out, and he clasped it. She squeezed but didn't let go.

Matt prayed again. In the course of twelve hours, his heart had become invested in this woman. He couldn't bear to see her like this. He felt the weight of helplessness all around him, like a fog that threatened to consume him.

Slowly, she pushed up. Gasps of air came loudly, searing his heart. He continued to rub her back until her breathing eased and she sat upright.

Kelly offered a tentative smile. "Thank you for coming."

He cleared his throat. "Of course. You want to sit at the table?"

She nodded, so he helped her up.

When Matt saw her pajama pants, he chuckled, and his shoulders shook. Pink background with unicorns and rainbows. He couldn't stop laughing. His earlier fright faded. As Kelly raised an eyebrow, he pointed to her pajama pants.

"Unicorns and rainbows."

She smiled. "You like them? They make me happy."

"They are so you," he said as his laughter subsided.

"So, how's your day going?" she asked with a wink.

"Better, now that you're okay. You are okay, right?"

She nodded, and the muscles in his shoulders unwound. "What triggered it?"

Kelly looked out the window. Her shoulders dipped with the weight of her anxiety.

"Mom said she gave Dad my address and number. He's going to be in town soon."

"Ah. And I take it you aren't exactly on speaking terms?"

She shook her head. "It's a long story."

Matt reached across the table and laced his fingers with hers.

"I've got time."

"It's not a story I want to tell right before I go to work."

"They must have updated their dress code," he quipped as he nodded toward her robe and pajama pants.

She snorted. "I won't leave for another hour and a half."

"Whew. You had me worried for a second."

The truth of those words hung thick in the air. How she dealt with the panic attacks so often was beyond him.

"I'm sorry. I'm sure I'm more than you bargained for."

She glanced down at their intertwined fingers and tried to pull away. He held her firm.

"Kelly, when I asked you out, I already knew about the panic attacks. I can't say they don't bother me. It's frightening, yeah. But I really care for you."

His heart might be farther gone. Not something to say aloud yet.

"No panic attack will change that."

"You're a brave man, Matt, to be interested in me. I'm a mess. A single mom who suffers from panic attacks, estranged from her father. So, so relationship with her mother. Most days, if it wasn't for God's grace, I'm not sure I could hold myself together at all."

Matt swallowed hard. "Then don't."

He patted his shoulder. "These shoulders are broad. Easy to lean on."

Kelly's eyes studied him for a long moment, her voice barely audible when she spoke. "Are you sure? You have so much on your plate already. Two jobs. Home group. A ministry. School."

"There's room for you." He would make room. He wanted to. More than anything ever.

A long sigh escaped her lips. "If you're sure…"

Matt stood and pulled her into his arms. He stroked his hand over her silky hair and held her for several minutes, savoring the warmth of her arms around his middle.

Yeah, his heart belonged to her already. No idea how it happened, but he was glad it did.

17

Kelly

A MONTH. KELLY smiled. She and Matt had been dating for nearly a month by the first Sunday in February, and it was growing stronger each day. They talked most days unless their schedules left no room. Friday and Saturday nights they usually spent together. At his place or out on a date. Rarely at her place alone. Too much temptation, he had said. She agreed.

She waved to him as she parked her car at the church. He jogged up to meet her. As he opened the car door for her, she beamed with a heart-warming smile. She loved his chivalry. After the door closed with a soft thud, he laced his fingers with hers.

"Morning," he said as he placed a kiss on her cheek. "Missed you."

Flutters started somewhere near her stomach and drifted up to her chest. She missed him, even though she had seen him on Friday night.

"How was the golf event?" he asked.

"Went off without a hitch, as far as the attendees knew." She winked at him. "We had one or two mishaps. Armando fixed an issue with the food. And Dwight knew a backup sound guy to cover for a no-show. He arrived only fifteen minutes later than when the music was supposed to start."

"My Kelly saved the day again."

She laughed. "I'm working with a great team. Thanks again for telling me about the job."

"It was meant to be."

When they entered the church lobby, Tori ran toward her and engulfed her in a hug as she squealed. Then Marcy and even Niki hugged her. Kelly finally felt like she belonged with the group of women. Joe and Chad gave their usual head nod. When Kyle joined them after dropping off Alana, he greeted her.

Matt stood next to her and handed her an iced caramel macchiato. The aroma of roasted beans filled the air as she took a sip. Perfect.

When Kelly glanced around the lobby, her eyes snagged on a familiar form. Her hand trembled and her heart pounded loudly. It couldn't be. What was *he* doing there? At *her* church?

Her throat constricted, and the wheezing sound came.

"Kelly? What is it?" Matt's deep voice sounded far away.

The man her eyes tracked disappeared into the crowd as her vision narrowed. Matt ducked into her line of sight.

"Look at me."

Her gaze fixed on Matt's. One hand settled at her waist. The other rested at the base of her neck. His thumb rubbed lines up the back of her neck, slowly easing the tension there.

Kelly sucked in a deep breath, confused. Her coffee. Had she dropped it?

"Tell me," Matt's whisper encouraged her.

"I thought... I thought I saw him."

Matt's raised eyebrow, coupled with his silence, made it clear she hadn't explained herself well.

"My dad."

Matt drew her close to his warm chest. "I'm sorry. I know your mom said he would be in town. Do you really think he would show up here?"

"I. Don't. Know."

"Okay. Take a deep breath for me."

Her shoulders lifted as air filled her lungs.

"Another?"

She did it again.

"Better?"

She closed her eyes and nodded her head against his neck, breathing in his calm comfort. Then she leaned back and offered a weak smile.

"I must be seeing things."

His lips brushed across her cheek before he released her. Then he turned and grabbed their coffees.

"You ready to go sit down?"

"Y-yes."

She accepted her coffee from his hand and gripped his arm to steady her shaky legs.

By the time they joined their friends, the lights had lowered, and the music began. Kelly eased into the seat, even though everyone else stood for the song. She needed another minute. Matt's hand felt reassuring and comforting on her shoulder.

She had to be seeing things. There was no way her father could be at her church. If he was, what were the odds they would end up in the same service? Nearly impossible.

For the second song, she stood and clasped Matt's hand as she sang softer than normal. Still, the music seeped deep into her soul as she offered worship to her Creator. Everything would be fine.

Once the music faded, she watched as Pastor Miles took the stage.

"Today it's my pleasure to introduce an old friend of mine, former pastor of a large church in Colorado Springs."

No. No. No. No. She shook her head as recognition dawned.

"Brent Sutton."

Kelly pushed past Matt and her friends, her breathing labored by the time she reached the aisle. She felt a wave of anxiety sweep over her, her chest tightening with each breath. She knew she couldn't make it out of the sanctuary, but she had to try. Air squeezed out of her lungs. Her vision swam and her knees buckled. She landed hard on the concrete stairs before sliding down at least two more. The church went silent except for the deafening pounding of her heart.

"Kelly!"

Matt?

18

Matt

MATT'S HEART LODGED in his throat when Kelly shoved him out of the way and took to the stairs. He scrambled over Joe, Chad, and Marcy in his haste to get to her, as perspiration dotted his forehead. Before he could reach her, she collapsed, hitting the stairs with a jarring thud. He watched in horror as she slid down a few stairs.

Please God.

The volunteer EMTs on staff during that service rushed to her side. The silence made their whispered words seem loud. At last, he reached Kelly.

"She has panic attacks," Matt spit out the words.

Sutton. Brent Sutton. Kelly Sutton. Her father.

The name finally registered, crashing over him. Matt's stomach clenched as he watched the EMTs examine Kelly. She looked too pale.

"Kelly?" An unfamiliar voice came from the aisle.

Matt's head snapped toward the man, and his shoulders twitched with barely restrained anger.

"That's my daughter."

Matt's jaw clenched tight as Brent Sutton reached for her hand.

"Give them space," he said gruffly. No way was he letting this man touch Kelly. If the mere sight of him could do this to her...

Brent's eyes widened before he raised his hands in surrender as he slowly backed away.

Paramedics arrived with a stretcher. The church volunteer EMTs relayed what they knew. One paramedic turned toward Matt.

"Are you family?"

He wished he was. Matt shook his head. "She's my girlfriend."

"I supposed it'd be alright if you rode with us."

Someone's voice came over the speakers and explained to the crowd what had happened. The worship pastor took the stage again. Soft, calming music filled the room as Matt took Kelly's hand in his. Then he released it while he ran beside the stretcher. The pounding of his feet on the hard sidewalk matched the frantic rhythm of his heart.

"Where are you taking her?" Brent asked behind him, his voice filled with concern.

"Chandler Regional," the paramedic answered.

"Where's that?" Brent asked.

None of them answered. Let someone else tell him. Not that Matt wanted him around Kelly. He didn't care if he didn't know the entire story. Anything that caused such a reaction in her triggered Matt's protectiveness. Until he heard from her lips that she wanted to see her father, the man would not get past Matt.

The paramedics swiftly loaded Kelly into the back of the ambulance, the sound of sirens echoing around them. As she turned her head towards him, her tears glistened in the light, trailing down her cheeks. The oxygen mask kept her from saying anything. Matt took her hand in both of his, his touch gentle and reassuring, a stark contrast to his own jumbled feelings.

Then he prayed silent words for her to heal, both physically and emotionally, from this shock. From whatever Brent Sutton did to her.

Quickly, the paramedics wheeled Kelly into the hospital, the smell of antiseptic filling the air. Matt stayed out of the way and followed every instruction from the hospital staff.

After what seemed like forever, they allowed him to see her.

"Matt."

His eyes burned at her hoarse voice. More than anything, he wished he could carry this for her.

"They want. More. Tests."

Tears dribbled down the side of her face, soaking the edge of the hospital gown.

"Told them. Panic attack."

"I'm sorry, honey." He leaned down and softly brushed a kiss on her forehead as his heart constricted.

"Please stay. Don't leave me."

"I won't." He wouldn't. Not a chance.

"I'm not crazy. I saw him." She broke eye contact.

"I'm sorry," Matt said. "When they mentioned his name at the staff meeting this week, I never made the connection. If I did, I would have told you."

She squeezed his hand. "Not your fault."

The words felt like a drop in the ocean compared to the flood of guilt consuming him.

His phone buzzed. Kyle.

How is she?

Matt texted him back she was alright, but he didn't know how long they would be at the hospital.

Tell her not to worry about Alana. I'll keep her with me until I hear otherwise.

"Kyle said he's got Alana and not to worry."

"Thank you."

Her eyelids drooped.

"Get some rest, Kel."

He breathed easier when her eyes closed and she relaxed.

Matt propped his elbows on his knees and dropped his head into his hands as the image of Kelly's body hitting the hard floor replayed over and over in his mind. The ache in his gut burrowed deeper. He felt so helpless. Useless. He wanted to protect her. But he had failed.

His phone dinged. Joe.

Every thing ok? Should we stop by?

Matt typed back: *Ok. Will be here for a while. Just pray.*

He snorted. Pray. It's what he ought to be doing instead of wallowing in self-pity.

As he leaned back in the chair by Kelly's side, he closed his eyes and expelled a loud breath. *Lord, please heal Kelly. Help the doctors to care for her. Help her not to dismiss their suggestions because she thinks she knows what this is.*

Matt stopped. It was a terrible prayer. Telling God what to do. Not like him.

Lord, I know You've got this. Help me release the need to control. Give me wisdom.

"Is she alright?"

Matt's eyes flew open, and his head jerked up to face Kelly's father. He jumped up and in two strides, took Brent Sutton's arm as he steered him out of the room.

"Don't you think you could have warned her?" he growled at the man.

Brent Sutton pointed his chin toward the visitor's waiting area. "Let's talk."

19

Matt

MATT FOLLOWED BEHIND Brent Sutton despite the anger churning in him. He needed to calm down.

Kelly's dad was a short man. Maybe five-foot-six. His dark eyes matched Kelly's. As he sat across from him, Matt noticed other similarities. The high cheekbones. The way he tapped his fingers on the side of his coffee mug. Kelly did that too.

"I'm Brent Sutton, Kelly's estranged father."

Matt snorted. Then he recovered and figured being nice would go far if he hoped to understand the rift between the two.

"Matt Dixon. Kelly's boyfriend."

Brent's chin dipped slowly in understanding.

"How much has she told you?"

"Why don't you give me your side of it?"

Brent cleared his throat as he fidgeted with the coffee mug in his hand.

"When Kelly was in high school, I had an affair with a member of the church I pastored. It started a few years before that. When Kelly was a junior, it became public. Very public."

Matt narrowed his eyes at the matter-of-fact way Brent described his adultery. Did he have any idea how much it hurt Kelly?

"Lisa and I had troubles long before then. That's Kelly's mother. So, when the affair became public, she divorced me quickly."

Brent looked down at his coffee, a frown wrinkling his brow.

"I don't blame her for it. She had every right to leave me. Anyway, the affair appeared in the newspapers and on the local TV channel. I lost my job at the church. During that time, I rarely spoke with Kelly. Partly because I was trying to pick up the pieces of my life and figure out what I could do for a living. And partly because Lisa threatened to file for sole custody if I upset Kelly."

He exhaled a heavy breath, and his shoulders drooped.

"In the end, it didn't matter. Kelly wanted nothing to do with me. Broke my heart. I never considered what my affair would do to her. I knew it would hurt Lisa, and I didn't care. But Kelly... I never meant for Kelly to get hurt."

"Seems naïve to me." Matt failed to keep the sharp edge from his voice.

"Maybe it was. Tell me, Matt, have you ever done something foolish when you were in love?"

He thought about something foolish right then, like letting his knuckles crack hard against Brent's cheekbone. Instead, he crossed his arms over his chest to keep from giving into the temptation.

Brent looked away. "She's never even met her sister, Audra. She's eleven."

Matt glowered at him wordlessly as his blood boiled.

"When Diana, the woman who I had the affair with, got pregnant, that's when everything came out. Audra was born a few months later. Since Lisa divorced me, I married Diana right away."

As he thought about it, Matt felt a low, dull ache in his gut. The man had been a pastor. A pastor. He had to have known better. When a man marries, he's not supposed to allow himself to fall in love with another woman. His wife should be his only love.

"I've never even met my granddaughter. Kelly refuses to

speak to me or return my calls."

"Why are you here, Brent? What do you think will happen?"

"I hope to reconcile with Kelly. I miss her and I want to be a part of her life. Of Alana's."

"Forcing her to see you here will not help. She's not ready to see you or talk to you. That much is obvious."

Brent let out a shaky breath. "You're right. I should go."

As Brent stood, he thrust a crumpled piece of paper at Matt. "Give her this. It's my number. When she's ready, I'd like to talk to her."

Matt snatched the paper from him and stuffed it in his pocket, narrowing his eyes in silent warning. He took a gulp of his coffee while he watched Brent leave.

What a mess, he thought before he returned to Kelly's side.

The afternoon dragged on as Matt sat in the chair and watched the hospital staff run more tests on Kelly. Finally, at seven in the evening, they discharged her to go home. Kyle had stopped by earlier to take Matt back to church to pick up his car, so he at least had it there.

Once Kelly sat in the passenger seat, he rounded to the other side and climbed behind the wheel. Some of the tension started unwinding from his shoulders.

"The hospital thought you shouldn't be alone. Do you want to go to my place?"

She shook her head. "I want to go home. And I don't want Alana to see me like this."

Matt sighed. He really wanted to stay with her, but didn't think he should. Not with no one else in the house.

"Please stay with me."

His resolve weakened at the pleading in her voice. His pulse raced. Staying with her was the last thing he ought to do.

"Matt, I need *you*. Not someone I barely know."

"Let's stop by my place so I can grab a few things." It

was a terrible idea. Joe would give him grief for it. Probably even try to stop him. Kyle, he wasn't so sure about.

But she needed him, so he would do it. Against his better judgment. Besides, the couch was downstairs. How much trouble could he get into as long as he stayed downstairs?

Once at his house, he packed his work laptop, his personal one, a change of clothes, and some grooming stuff. Then he hurried out the door before Joe spotted him. He told Kyle he would be back tomorrow.

Then he drove Kelly home. When she wanted to rest on the couch, he made sure she was comfortable before he ordered delivery. His stomach growled as he waited for the food to arrive.

Kelly slept through the delivery, so he ate and stowed the rest in the fridge for later. Then he turned on his computer and tried to do some schoolwork. Around eleven, the stress of the day sapped his energy. He shut it off before walking over to the couch.

"Hey." He nudged Kelly.

As she stirred and smiled up at him, her gaze filled with love. His heart melted, and he ignored the warning in his gut.

"Let's get you upstairs. You'll be more comfortable."

Kelly stood. When she took a step, she swayed, so he helped her upstairs. Once she was in bed, he flipped off the lights and turned to leave.

"Stay with me?"

Matt's pulse shot off like a rocket. Whoa there. She wasn't asking for intimacy. Just comfort. That thought failed to calm him.

"I don't think it's a good idea."

"Please. It's been a long day. I feel so alone."

He let out a shaky breath and reclined next to her on top of the blankets. Not that blankets would make a difference. Then he looped his arm around her waist and breathed in her sweet strawberry fragrance. The warmth of her body next to his sent his mind spinning. Thoughts of waking up with her. Of a home with her. He had to get a grip.

When her breathing shallowed, he hurried from the room, doing his best not to wake her. Then he changed into something more comfortable and laid on the couch alone. Downstairs. Away from temptation.

Sometime around two in the morning, he shot upright, suddenly awake. His pulse raced when he heard Kelly's cry.

"Matt!"

He ran up the stairs two at a time and burst through the door. His heart broke when he saw her tear-streaked face in the dim light from her bedside lamp.

"I thought you left me alone."

He knew that feeling too well, thanks to his father. His shoulders sagged as he itched to comfort her.

"I'm sorry, Kel. So sorry."

Then he climbed into bed next to her and held her in his arms. Her body shook with sobs, so he caressed her silky hair and murmured loving words to her.

When Kelly calmed, she looked up at him. Her brown eyes begged him to stay. All he could focus on was the softness of her lips and the desire to taste them. He stared at her for a long moment. Then he lowered his lips to hers.

She swiftly pressed her warm body against him, returning his kiss eagerly. In the far recesses of his mind, he knew he should jump out of the bed and put some distance between them. It was too dangerous to stay. Except she felt so perfect in his arms. So eager for his kisses and his touch.

One thing led to another. They tossed aside clothes, along with any hint of morality. By mutual consent, he made love to her sweetly. Passionately. Hoping Kelly saw his heart and how much he loved her.

20

Kelly

KELLY WOKE FEELING well-rested. Matt's warmth comforted her. She snuggled close to him as she remembered what happened at two in the morning. Guilt tried to surface but she pushed it down.

She loved him. This. Him being there felt perfect. She hadn't intended to go there with Matt before marriage. But they had.

When she cupped his face in her hand, his eyes flashed open, revealing the full impact of her touch. He grabbed her wrist.

"Kelly."

Despite the warning in his husky voice, she gazed into his eyes. Smoldering. Thrilling.

Then he rolled onto his back as he clenched the sheets in his fisted hands. Tension radiated from him as intense as the midday sun in the height of summer.

After several minutes of silence, he said, "Kelly, I'm sorry. I shouldn't have done that. I should have had more self- control last night."

Kelly placed a finger on his lips. "Hush. We both wanted it. We both let it happen. Don't cheapen it."

He relaxed and rolled onto his side, carefully pinning the blankets between them. Then he brushed the hair back from her face.

"Cheapen? That's the last thing I want you to feel about what just happened. I..." His Adam's apple bobbed before he spoke again. "I love you, Kelly."

"I love you too, Matt." And she did.

When his tender expression vanished, her heart plummeted.

"But we can't do this. We're not married. We shouldn't do this."

Then he threw back the covers and gathered his things before he bolted out of her bedroom. The chilly rejection caused her to shiver.

"Come down for breakfast when you're... decent," he hollered from halfway down the stairs.

Kelly fell back against her pillow as a tear trailed down her cheek. He was right. They shouldn't have.

She felt the wave of reality hitting her, as if it had physical weight. She had just made the same mistake again. How many friendships with men did she have to destroy before she learned her lesson?

As she left the warmth of her bed behind, she hopped into the shower. When the warm water flowed over her back, she sobbed. No fleeting moment of bliss was worth the pain crushing her heart now.

How could she have been so reckless?

Would Matt break up with her over this? She hoped not, but she couldn't shake off her fear.

Things had been going so well between them. They had been happy. They had been building something good.

She turned off the water and toweled off. Steam clouded the mirror, just like sorrow clouded her heart.

When she finished grooming, she padded downstairs, only to find Matt had left. Fear constricted her throat until she noticed his backpack on a chair at the table. He had to come back for it. Maybe she could fix this.

Kelly brewed herself a cup of coffee. At the sound of the door opening behind her, she started a cup for him, the nutty aroma failing to perk her up.

Quietly, he dropped some grocery bags on the counter.

She slid a warm cup of coffee toward him as she planned what she could say to save them. Because she desperately didn't want this one mistake to end them.

21

Matt

MATT SHOWERED DOWNSTAIRS, scolding himself the entire time. He knew better. He *knew* better than that. It was his responsibility to keep that from happening, and he had failed. He took advantage of her fragile feelings.

No, that wasn't entirely true. She consented.

Still, he should never have spent the night in her home, much less in her bed. He should have listened to the warning about his self-control. Yeah, what self-control? Seemed he had none.

After he ran a towel over his damp hair, he donned his fresh clothes. Then he picked up after himself. He tossed the wet towel in the laundry room and stashed his dirty clothes in his bag, all the while kicking himself for going there with Kelly.

Without protection, too.

He was some kind of idiot on so many levels. Not nearly the man of integrity he claimed to be.

Brent's words chose that moment to emerge from his memory. *Have you ever done something foolish for love?*

Um. Yeah. Everything since leaving the hospital with Kelly.

His muscles wound tight, and he needed to do something. Breakfast. He should make breakfast. Kelly had some food on hand, though a trip to the store might do him more good. Matt found a piece of paper and jotted a quick note to let her know he would be back in a few minutes.

Then he grabbed his keys and hurried into the cool morning.

Monday. Work. He sighed.

Before he pulled out of the parking lot, he texted his boss to let him know he would work from home and start a little late. As soon as he finished cooking breakfast for Kelly, he would go home and log on.

Once at the store, Matt bought some bacon and eggs. A few fresh ingredients. Then he headed down *that* aisle. The one with 'family planning' items. His faced heated. The last thing he needed was for someone to see him buying condoms. Still, if he couldn't get a grip on his self-control, it would be better to have some.

His stomach churned as he swiped a box from the shelf and stuffed it under other things in his basket. Then he hastened to the self-checkout. He glanced around nervously as he slid the box over the scanner. If the youth pastor, or any of the youth, or anyone, really, caught him purchasing those... He didn't want to think about the repercussions.

As soon as he paid for his purchase, he dashed out of the store, heat flaming his neck and face. He was the absolute worst boyfriend. He should have already been prepared, just in case. Or he should have stopped himself. Or he should have never stayed at Kelly's place to begin with.

Maybe his father had been right. Maybe he had deserved what the vile man dished out. He certainly didn't deserve mercy or grace. Not for this insurmountable mistake.

When Matt parked his car, he sat in it for a few minutes to gather himself. He left *the* box in his car. Then he tried to quiet all the voices that accused him of being a hypocrite, a fool, an idiot.

Shoulders squared, he entered Kelly's home. She smiled and fixed him a coffee. Then she sat at the bar while he cooked bacon and omelets.

He didn't look at her. He couldn't. Not when he failed her so massively.

Thankfully, while he focused on cooking at the stove, his back faced the bar.

"As soon as breakfast is done, I have to go to work. Well, home to work."

"Thank you for staying last night. It meant a lot to me."

He snorted. The smell of bacon filled the air as he turned over the strips. His stomach clenched.

"Matt."

After he cracked eggs into a bowl, he yanked open several drawers, slamming them closed until he found a whisk.

"Matt."

Focusing on his task, he attacked the eggs with the whisk, the sound of metal against ceramic ringing in the quiet room. At least they would be fluffy.

Kelly sighed loudly and groaned. "Just great. My last boyfriend broke up with me because I wouldn't have sex with him. Now you're gonna break up with me because I did."

The whisk caught on the edge of the bowl and dropped to the tile floor with a clatter. Drops of egg pooled under the utensil. Matt left it as he poured the eggs into the pan, and then he whirled around to face her.

"I'm not breaking up with you!" He scowled at her.

"Sure feels like it from here."

"Unless you want me to?" Insecurity and doubt hovered over him like a black monsoon cloud waiting to pour more recrimination into his heart.

Kelly slid from the bar stool. When she stood next to him, she rubbed a hand on his back.

"I don't want you to."

"Good. 'Cause I don't want to either. But I can't... I can't talk about it right now."

Her voice softened. "Okay. I just wanted to make sure you knew how much your support and presence meant to me yesterday. At the hospital."

Matt glanced at the eggs and folded them over, just like he learned as a line cook during his summer job in high school.

"Got some plates?"

She scooted around him to a cupboard nearby and retrieved them. Then Matt placed an omelet and several strips of bacon on each.

"I bought some orange juice. Would you mind?"

Kelly poured two glasses and carried them to the table, along with the silverware. She cleared a space for them to eat.

When he brought over the plates, he set one in front of her, still not making eye contact. How could he? He failed her so badly.

Neither said a word throughout the meal, not even a blessing over it. Tally up another failure on his part. When they finished, he jammed his laptop into his backpack. Then he stormed toward the door without a word.

"Matt, will you be okay?" Kelly asked.

"Give me a few days."

Then he tugged the door open and headed home as the guilt chased him like a pack of wolves.

When Matt arrived, Joe was there. Just his luck.

"How's Kelly?"

"Fine."

Matt pushed past him to his bedroom.

"Really?"

"I said she's fine," Matt snapped, as he tossed his backpack on his bed with a thud.

"Bro, what's got you in a fury?"

"I gotta log on for work."

A few minutes later, he heard the garage door open. Then, a minute later, Joe fumed back into the house. He tossed the box of condoms on Matt's desk.

"What is this?"

Matt swiveled his chair to look at his friend as his gut

twisted. "What do you think it is? Why are you going through my car?"

"I wasn't. I set my coffee on your hood and when I picked it up, I saw this on the passenger seat."

"And?"

Joe cleared his throat. "Bro, I thought we agreed to hold each other accountable. About drinking. About…"

Guilt churned Matt's stomach. Joe was right. The two of them agreed to that years ago. They had had one or two tough conversations over the years. Nothing that compared to the one Joe started then.

"Did you and Kelly…"

Matt's gaze darted away from his friend as he crossed his arms over his chest. He couldn't face the disappointment in his friend's eyes.

Joe's voice softened when he spoke. "Bro, this is serious. You can't keep working at church."

Matt's head jerked toward him as his pulse raced. "What happens in my relationship with Kelly is nobody's business."

"You and I both know that isn't true. Especially when you're working with a bunch of impressionable teens."

The words sliced through him because he knew they were true.

"I'm not gonna say anything, but I think you should step down."

Matt's jaw tightened. Just like that. With one night of weakness, he destroyed his life.

22

Kelly

ON WEDNESDAY AFTERNOON, Kelly texted Kyle asking him to pick up Alana. She had to work late for a last-minute business meeting in the ballroom. The guests had paid extra, but that didn't help her schedule. At least it didn't happen often.

Sure thing. Kyle texted back.

Now for the tougher text. Matt.

They hadn't spoken since he left Monday morning. No call. No text. Now she had to let him know she wouldn't be at home group. No opportunity to talk to him before or after.

As her eyes burned, she sent a prayer heavenward.

Lord, I know we should have waited. I'm sorry. I'm sorry I made Matt feel pressured. Please, don't let this be the end of us. I love him.

Kelly sank into her office chair as the tears rolled down her cheeks. She meant it all. If she had any idea how going there would have affected Matt, she would have been stronger.

After drying her eyes, she tried to call Matt. No answer.

"Matt, it's me. We really need to talk, but I have to work tonight. Can you call me, please?" *I love you.*

She texted him, too. Then she dropped her phone into her nice purse, and slung it over her shoulder.

Kelly hurried down the hall with purpose, the sound of her heels echoing on the stone tile. The facility manager smiled a warm greeting, and they quickly reviewed the setup for the evening's event. Once it started, Chef Foley assigned a server to refill beverages. The sound guy oversaw audio, video, and lights. She hovered nearby, in case the meeting organizers needed anything.

When she glanced at her watch, she yawned. Nine. She checked her phone and saw a text from Alana. A pang of guilt pricked her conscience. She hated missing texts from her daughter. Maybe someday she could work a job with normal hours. Or not have to work at all and stay home to take care of children.

Heat warmed her cheeks as the memories from early Monday morning came to mind. Then she realized they hadn't used protection. Crud. Stupid. Would she ever learn not to repeat the same mistakes? Kelly resolved to pick up a pregnancy test that weekend. Though it was the last thing she or Matt needed, it would help set aside her fears if she knew for certain.

"Miss Sutton?" Jake, the meeting organizer, waved her down. He explained he was looking for some notepaper and pens. He forgot to bring enough for the last activity of the night.

Kelly quickly stood and jogged back to her office. She grabbed a pack of notepaper and a box of pens before she returned to the meeting. Then she sat in the back while Jake explained the activity to the attendees.

While she waited, she glanced at her phone again. No voicemails. No texts from Matt. Silence. He was ghosting her. She felt it through the deep ache in her chest.

When the attendees finally left the ballroom, Kelly felt more anxious about Matt. It was far too late to stop by his place. She could make an excuse about wanting to pick up Alana, but there was no point in waking her. Let her get a good night's sleep before school in the morning. Kyle already texted he planned to take her.

Still, as she climbed into her car and drove home, she wished she could hear Matt's voice or see his face. Something to get clarity on the state of their relationship.

23

Matt

MATT GLANCED AT his phone. Eleven-thirty. Too late to call Kelly. Too late to stop by.

He snorted. Stopping by her place was the very last thing he should do, especially late at night. He didn't trust himself.

Guilt piled on top of shame. He needed to talk to her. To clear the air. He didn't want to break up with her, but he needed to tell her how he felt and not just about her. He needed to tell her why everything bothered him so much.

At least he thought he knew why it bugged him. He wanted to be better than the younger version of himself who had drowned his feelings in alcohol. He wanted to be different from his father. Most of all, he didn't want to preach one message to the youth group while he failed so miserably to save himself for marriage.

Even though he sowed his wild oats before becoming a Christian, he vowed he would live a pure life from that point until his wedding night. He shook his head. He had obliterated that boundary on Monday early morning.

Still, he and Kelly could recommit to celibacy for the duration of the relationship, until they were married. If their relationship led to marriage. Maybe he had already blown any chance of that.

Matt stood and ran a hand through his hair. He needed to talk to Kelly.

He picked up his phone and texted her.

Any chance you're still up?

A few seconds later, the answer came back.

Just got home.

He punched the button to call her.

"Hey." Her sweet voice gave him hope.

"Sorry we haven't been able to connect," he said.

"I know you have a lot on your plate."

Guilt hounded him again. Truthfully, he had been ghosting her for two days.

"Kelly, I... How are you feeling?"

"You mean from Sunday? Okay. If you mean us, I'm worried."

"I love you, Kelly. I'm not so shallow to go there with you without loving you."

"I love you, Matt Dixon. Don't ghost me." Her voice cracked. "Too many people have done that to me. I couldn't bear it if you did."

"I'm sorry." He was. "Do you think we can move past this? Recommit to not having sex?"

"I... I think so."

Silence lingered for several seconds.

"Matt? I'm sorry I pressured you. I feel horrible."

"I'm supposed to lead you, Kel. To be more godly, not... Not that. I failed you."

"All is forgiven."

His eyes burned. Yet another reason to love this woman.

A yawn came across the line. "It's late. When are you free again?"

"Friday evening. I've got youth tomorrow." Unless he confessed to the youth pastor like Joe suggested.

"As of right now, I'm free, too. We don't have any conferences scheduled for the weekend, so that shouldn't change."

"Why don't you come over here? I'll cook for you, Alana, Kyle, and Joe. Tori, if she's free. Then you and I can go for a walk or something?"

"Sounds good."

After they said their goodbyes, Matt hung up his phone, relieved that they finally talked. They would be alright. No one had to know they had slipped up. Joe knew, but he would keep quiet. He and Kelly would move forward with more self-control. Intentionally, not being alone in a tempting situation. He would make sure of it.

24

Kelly

FRIDAY AFTERNOON, KELLY loaded Alana in the car after daycare. Then she went to the grocery store to shop for the week. She preferred shopping with Alana to make sure she bought things her daughter would eat. It didn't always work out that way because she shared custody with Kyle. Since she was going over to Matt's, it made more sense for her to bring Alana to Kyle instead of him picking her up.

After several minutes in the cereal aisle, Alana finally decided on something for breakfast for the coming week. Just before they left the aisle, Alana dashed back and retrieved a second box. Kelly smiled. She figured Alana wanted both.

When they walked past the drugstore section of the store, Kelly slowed down. She felt her heart pounding against her ribcage. She needed to buy a test.

"Sweetie, why don't you look at some hair accessories while I pick up a couple of things?"

Taking advantage of the distraction, Kelly made her way quickly to the aisle with the pregnancy tests. She selected one at random and threw it in the basket. Then she caught up to Alana.

"Find something you like?"

She nodded and held out bright pink ponytail holders. Kelly dropped them in the cart and they finished shopping.

Once at home, Alana packed up her tablet, the new ponytail holders, and a few other things in her backpack while Kelly unloaded the groceries. Alana was ready, but Kelly hurried upstairs and took the pregnancy test.

The seconds ticked by ever so slowly. When the timer on her phone buzzed, she glanced at the test. She gripped the sink with both hands as her stomach lurched, the surface cold and smooth on her fingertips.

Positive.

Would she ever learn from her past mistakes?

Pregnant. Again.

She turned on the bathroom fan to muffle her guttural moan. What should be joyful news tore a gaping hole through her heart. Another child. A baby. As if her life wasn't complicated enough.

What would Matt say? What would he do?

Kelly shook her head. Maybe she should take another test before she said anything to him. With the way he reacted on Monday…

"Mommy?" Alana's voice came from the other side of the door.

"Just a minute, sweetie."

Kelly took a few deep breaths. She stared at her reflection as she recalled Kyle's reaction when she told him she had been pregnant with Alana. Stoic. Angry. He had rejected her. It was the end of their friendship. Apart from having the child support taken out of his paycheck, he did nothing else to help her. Then last year, he showed up out of the blue, finally ready to be a dad. None of the good he did in the last year took away the pain of his initial rejection. She hadn't expected him to marry her. That would have been two wrongs. But to withdraw friendship? Leave her so alone? Not to be part of Alana's life. He abandoned her when she needed a friend the most.

As she straightened her shoulders, she hoped Matt's reaction would be better. She had to tell him. Right away. If she didn't, it would eat her alive. Possibly trigger frequent panic attacks again. It might be the end of their friendship.

The death of their budding relationship.

She shook her head. It was the right thing to do. Regardless of the risk, she would tell him that night. Let the chips fall where they may.

Plastering on a smile that didn't match her feelings, Kelly opened the bathroom door.

"Thanks for waiting, sweetie. Ready?"

When her daughter nodded, Kelly ushered them out to the car. She turned on the music for the car ride to Matt's, mostly to drown out the noise in her mind.

Another child. Matt's child.

She chewed the inside of her lip. He wouldn't ask her to terminate it, would he? She couldn't do that. Never. It was against everything she believed. Surely he believed the same, didn't he?

When her eyes burned, she gripped the steering wheel so tight her knuckles turned white. What if Matt wanted nothing to do with her or the baby? Would he reject her like every other man had? Derek, Kyle, her father.

That thought threatened her composure. Her father never pursued joint custody of her. One day, they were a family. The next, they weren't. His affair had become public. Her mother kicked him out of their house, slapped him with a divorce, and that was it. Her father was gone. The heaviness in her chest threatened to squeeze all the air from her lungs.

After the birth of his second daughter, — Kelly cringed over the word — he finally reached out. Mom told him to go to court if he wanted to change the custody arrangement. He didn't. He had his new family. His new daughter. He didn't need or want Kelly anymore.

"Mommy, you went past it."

"Sorry."

She pulled into the closest driveway and turned around, paying attention that time. When she turned off the car, the crushing weight of her circumstances prevented her from getting out; all she heard was the ticking of the engine cooling down.

"You go on in. I'll be right there."

Alana jumped out of the car and bounded up the stairs to the front porch. Kelly watched to make sure someone let her in. Then she pretended like she needed to pick up the contents of her purse, stalling. She was not ready for the serious conversation ahead of her. She didn't know if she could trust Matt to be a father to her baby.

25

Matt

"WHERE'S YOUR MOTHER?" Matt heard Kyle ask Alana.

"She said she would be in."

Matt frowned as his chest tightened. That didn't bode well.

"Was she wheezing?" he asked.

"No. Just sad."

Alana squeezed Kyle's neck, effectively ending the conversation.

Matt dried his hands on a towel and rushed toward the door. Just as he opened it, Kelly flung open her car door. When she saw him, she flinched. Not good. He should have talked to her sooner. Not ghosted her.

He held the front door wide as she entered his home. Then he kissed her cheek. When she finally smiled, he started breathing again. Maybe he had read into her reaction. She might be fine.

"Tori is gonna join us for dinner. Hope that's okay," he said.

"That will be nice."

"I'm just finishing up in the kitchen. Joe will be in shortly with the steaks. You want to set the table?"

"Sure."

When her eyes flicked away from him quickly, his stomach clenched. Matt thought she would be happier to see him. He thought they left things in a decent place when they talked on Wednesday. Guess he had read that wrong.

Maybe she planned to break up with him after all. Didn't want to be around a hypocrite like him. The thought of losing her nearly doubled him over. Their connection had been strong. Life changing. And he ruined it all by not leading like he should have. Not maintaining self-control.

He squared his shoulders and mentally shook off the oppressively dark thoughts. Maybe she just had a long day at work and it had nothing to do with him. That was a real possibility. Right?

"Hello!" Tori's voice came from the entryway. "This is a pleasant treat."

She gave hugs to everyone before asking Kyle if Niki was coming.

"She and Marcy are wedding planning."

"Shouldn't you be involved?" Tori asked.

"Marcy told me to make myself scarce."

Tori laughed as she held the back door open for Joe, since his hands were full.

Matt glanced at Kelly. She looked down at the table. Not the least hint of laughter. The corners of her mouth turned downward and her eyes reddened. An ominous chill ran through his body. Something was very wrong.

"What's so funny?" Joe asked.

Matt finished making the pasta salad, ignoring the jabs at Kyle's expense. He had to make things right with Kelly. Whatever it took. It was his failure. His responsibility. He would own it and help her see that.

A hand on his back caused him to jump.

"Sorry," Kelly said.

"I didn't hear you."

Matt stirred the dressing into the pasta salad. The aroma should have made his mouth water. Instead, it went dry as he dodged Kelly's gaze.

"I asked if you need help."

"I got it. Wanna get drinks for everyone?"

When she didn't move, he met her gaze. Soul-shattering

sorrow. Not good at all.

"I missed you," she said. Then she kissed his cheek and spun away.

Matt sighed. He hated the awkward distance between them. The mixed signals. He couldn't shake the feeling of impending doom despite her claim of missing him.

When everyone sat at the table, Matt didn't have it in him to pray. Instead, he asked Kyle, who responded with raised eyebrows.

"Of course."

Matt reached for Kelly's hand. She took it. That was a positive sign. He hoped.

When the prayer finished, they passed around the food. Kyle loaded a plate for Alana.

"That's too much," Kelly said, her brows drawn.

Kyle grinned. "I'm just loading her plate with seconds for me."

Kelly rolled her eyes as she took the pasta salad and dropped a tiny spoonful on her own plate. When she chose the smallest steak and just a little green salad, Matt became more concerned. She normally had a decent appetite.

Maybe he should have suggested they go out to talk instead. He just didn't want to have a serious conversation about their future in a noisy restaurant.

Throughout the meal, neither he nor Kelly said much. She pushed the food around on her plate, eating only a few bites. Tension coiled around his heart, squeezing the life from it.

As soon as they finished the meal, he stood and helped clear the table.

"We'll get this," Joe said as he nodded in Kelly's direction. "You two are overdue for a conversation."

"Thanks, bro."

Kelly stood and stepped onto the back patio, with Matt following behind. He stopped short when he noticed her arms wrapped around her middle. After he closed the sliding glass door, he stood next to her, staring out at the yard in the waning sunlight.

"I thought we left things in a good place on Wednesday. You seem out of sorts," he said as he kicked a rock off the patio.

Kelly snorted. "We did."

Then she turned toward him. "I am out of sorts."

As he turned to face her, she seemed to fold into herself. Her eyes glistened in the low light and her lip trembled.

"I'm pregnant."

26

Matt

THE WORDS TOOK several seconds to register in Matt's brain. Then he stumbled backward a few steps as if she had punched him in the gut. Bile crawled up the back of his throat.

Pregnant.

"It's only been a few days. How can you know already?" He folded his arms over his chest as he tried to let the reality sink in. The implications. A child. With Kelly. It changed everything.

She stepped closer. "They have these things called pregnancy tests, Matt. I took one. Right before coming over here."

He swallowed hard. "Is it accurate?"

"It was right the last time."

Matt uncrossed his arms. "Is it too soon to know for sure?"

"Look, if you don't want to be a part of this baby's life, then just say so. I managed on my own last time. I'll be fine without you!"

"Kel, that's not fair. I just found out you're pregnant thirty seconds ago. I don't know what to say or how it works." *Or what to do.*

"Mommy?"

His head snapped toward the sliding glass door where Alana stood holding it open. The muscle in his jaw twitched. The sweet little girl looked scared. Then his eyes shot to the people behind her. Tori's eyes widened before she skulked out of view. Joe frowned and shook his head as his shoulders slumped. Kyle recovered from his shock and reached for the open door.

"Come on, Pumpkin. Let's leave your mommy to talk to Matt. We'll watch the movie without her."

"It's alright," Kelly's voice changed to sugary sweet. "You go enjoy the movie with your daddy."

Alana's eyes remained round as Kyle led her back inside and closed the sliding glass door with a soft thud. Matt's stomach dropped to the ground. Joe turned away, but not before Matt registered his disgust.

He ran a hand through his hair before he paced the length of the porch.

Pregnant. He was going to be a father.

The word "father" felt more oppressive than the word "pregnant." His dad been the worst kind of father. What if he was just as bad?

When Kelly shuffled toward the sliding door, Matt's mind raced. He needed a plan, and fast. One that would keep Kelly from bolting out the door or withdrawing from him.

"Let's go for a walk," he suggested. Movement would help him. Hopefully, her too.

"Fine." Her terse reply sliced through his heart.

He held his breath as he opened the sliding glass door. She ducked under his arm, keeping her head down as she scampered toward the front door.

"We're going for a walk," he announced without looking at anyone as he tried to catch up to her.

When he reached for her hand, she allowed him to lace his fingers with hers. He blew out a loud breath. That was a good sign. He set a leisurely pace towards the community park, taking in the sound of birds chirping in the trees.

"First, let me say," Matt started, "that we should one hundred percent keep this child. That was not in question, but I want you to know where I stand."

Kelly released a loud breath. "Agreed."

"Second, I'll need some time to think about a long-term plan. It's a shock."

Complete and total shock. The last thing he had ever expected. Such a life-altering consequence from one fleeting, passionate moment. His life would never be the same. Nor Kelly's. Nor the baby's or Alana's. His failure had affected many people.

A sob escaped Kelly's throat, and he stopped, turning toward her.

"It's a shock to me, too. I can't believe I've done it again."

Matt pulled her against his chest and wrapped his arms around her. The warmth from her body did little to comfort him. He stroked her soft hair as she sobbed against his shirt, damp circles forming over his heart. A few tears leaked from his eyes, too. Tears of remorse. Of fear. Of sorrow.

When she calmed down, he suggested they keep walking to the park. Once there, they sat on a bench and he placed an arm around her. A dog's frenetic bark echoed in the chilly night air, mirroring the anxiety in his heart.

He rubbed his hand on her smooth arm while he tried to reason out his next move. Marriage? Was that the right thing?

They hadn't known each other long. Sure, he felt closer to Kelly than any woman he had ever met. There was something deep between them. More than just attraction. A heart connection. Maybe even more.

But marriage? They barely knew each other. If he married her, it would be for life. Before he could ask her, he must make sure he was ready to honor lifelong vows. Divorce was not an option in his mind. It went against everything he believed.

So did sleeping with his girlfriend before marriage. He snorted and shook his head in disgust.

When Kelly straightened her back, he knew he had to open his mouth and tell her something. Anything. Talk it out.

"Is it right to offer marriage?" he asked. "'Cause I will, Kelly. I love you, and that will not change. Marriage seems like a big step sooner than I expected. But I think we could absolutely make it work."

At least he hoped they could. Had he really just said he loved her? Maybe he did. Maybe his heart knew more than his brain.

"I... I don't know. We've only been dating for five weeks."

Five weeks. A lump formed in his constricting throat.

"Let's not rush into it," Kelly said. "I'm not saying no. But I think we both need to think about it."

Prayer. They ought to pray about it too. Except the word wouldn't make it past his lips. Guilt held it back.

"I'll have to step down from everything at church." The realization crushed him. Church. Seminary. Incomplete goals. Lost dreams.

Kelly stiffened next to him. "Just like..."

"This is not like your father. He had an affair and was the senior pastor."

"Matt, people... Blamed Mom. They blamed me."

He frowned. Who blames a teenager for her parents' failures?

"Our closest friends will know." He snorted. "Looks like they already know. I'll talk to Pastor Miles and Pastor Chris alone. They won't let it spread. They'll tell the youth that I'm stepping down for personal reasons."

Kelly groaned. "Until everyone sees me in a few months."

He hated himself for the pain his failure brought on her. How could he have been so selfish? So stupid. So out of control. This wasn't her fault. It was his. All his.

"Kelly, let me bear that burden. I will not leave you

alone in this, no matter what we decide about marriage. I will be here for you. For the baby."

He rested his head against the top of hers and held her closer, breathing deeply of her sweet fragrance. He closed his eyes, which forced a trail of moisture to roll down his cheek.

He was about to become a father. A tiny life depended on him to act responsibly. Kelly needed him to do the right thing. If only he could figure out what that was.

Seminary seemed completely useless at that point. Even if he wanted to go into ministry full time, it was no longer an option. He should withdraw. Let it go. On Monday, he would see to it. In fact, he might just take a few days off work too. He had plenty of vacation time. Might not hurt to deal with things quickly.

"I'm sorry," Kelly said.

"Hush now. This is on me. I failed you."

Matt coughed to clear his throat.

"Should you go to the doctor?" he asked. "I really do not know what happens next."

"I could get confirmation through a blood test. Except I haven't even established a doctor here yet."

Guilt squeezed his gut. She had already dealt with so much in the last few months. Now this.

"We'll figure it out." Somehow. "Together."

After she wilted against him, Matt did the best he could to comfort her despite his own shattered heart. They sat that way in silence for a long time. When she shivered, he walked her back to her car. She wanted to be alone at home, so he watched her drive away.

The door opened behind him, and he turned to face a furious Joe.

27

Matt

"I WARNED YOU, didn't I?"

Matt narrowed his eyes at Joe. His best friend's words made him feel a wave of rage and he suddenly felt an urge to swing at him.

"Your self-righteousness isn't helpful."

Joe scoffed. "I told you she was on the rebound. That you were playing with fire."

Matt stepped closer.

"Yes, Joe, you did. You tried to warn me."

Then he shoved his friend.

"So what do you want me to say? I screwed up? Because I did. Big time."

Joe shook his head. "I'm so disappointed. I thought out of all of us, you'd be the strongest."

The words pulverized Matt's already broken heart. He had never been strong. Not like Joe. Not like Chad. Even when he thought he had himself together, he knew how deceitful his heart truly was.

Joe let out a long sigh. "What are you gonna do?"

That was better. Friendship. Concern. That's what he needed right then.

"I don't know. Guess I've got the weekend to think about it."

"I'm sorry."

Matt wasn't sure if Joe was apologizing for his attitude or for Matt's failure. Didn't matter. He needed someone in his corner.

"Alana is in bed. Tori left. So if you want to talk, it's just me and Kyle. We'll listen."

Matt nodded as Joe opened the door. He followed his friend inside. A part of him wanted to isolate. To hide from his friends. He knew that might not be the best idea. So he flopped down on the couch and talked.

"I just read this today and I think it might help," Kyle said as he tapped a few times on his phone. "Do not fear, for I have redeemed you; I have summoned you by name; you are mine. When you pass through the waters, I will be with you; and when you pass through the rivers, they will not sweep over you. When you walk through the fire, you will not be burned; the flames will not set you ablaze. For I am the Lord your God, the Holy One of Israel, your Savior."

Joe nodded. "God will be with you, Matt. You know this. Even though the consequences of your sin feel like deep waters ready to sweep you away, if you seek Him, He will help you."

They were right. Despite his sins and the consequences, Matt could still confess and seek God's direction for what came next. Marriage. Job. School. All of it was in God's hands. If he humbled himself and asked for forgiveness, God would be merciful. Of course, He wouldn't take away the consequences of Matt's sin, but He would forgive him.

Matt thanked them and headed to his room. After he shut the door and flipped off the light, he climbed into his bed. While he stared at the ceiling, he poured out his failures and regrets to the Creator of his soul. He confessed his lack of self-control. He owned his actions. And he laid it all before God Almighty. When he finished the prayer, he let go of his self-recrimination. Peace still eluded him, but he trusted God would help him navigate the mess he had made.

28

Kelly

KELLY PULLED INTO her parking spot at home and rested her head on the steering wheel, grateful Kyle had Alana over the weekend. She needed a minute. Or a day. Or two to sort out her feelings and to face reality.

She felt nauseous and dizzy. She couldn't believe she had made the same mistake. Again.

After all the times Derek had pressured her for intimacy, she had stood strong. Didn't give in. Held on to her convictions.

Then, after one encounter with her estranged father, the resulting panic attack, and her frayed nerves, she had manipulated Matt into her bed. She didn't deserve to be a mother. She was too irresponsible.

Her phone pinged, so she leaned back in her seat as her shoulders slumped.

I only live a few minutes away. Got some Ben & Jerry's if you need a friend. Tori.

Kelly pushed open the door of her car and trudged into her home as she warred over whether to take Tori up on her offer. Before she could chicken out, she texted back "yes" with her address.

While she waited for Tori, she ran upstairs and changed into her funny unicorns and rainbows pajama pants and a soft t-shirt. Then she returned to the living room and crashed onto the couch.

A few minutes later, Tori rang the doorbell. Kelly stood

and let her in.

Tori held up a very full bag. "I brought six flavors. I think you should be able to find one that you like."

Kelly retrieved two spoons from the drawer and handed one to Tori. After Tori set the ice cream on the counter, Kelly picked her favorite, as did Tori. Then they put the rest in the freezer and sat on opposite ends of the big couch.

She popped off the top and scraped a big spoonful into her mouth. Closing her eyes, she savored the creamy, sweet chocolate. The cool ice cream felt like a soft blanket over her battered heart.

"So..." Tori said. "Rough day?"

Kelly snorted. "Rough year."

Then she poured out her troubles to her new friend. Tori listened, which was all Kelly really needed. Someone to let her talk out her jumbled mess of feelings.

"Matt offered marriage," she said.

"Not surprised. That's the kind of guy he is."

"I just don't know. I love him. That's about the only thing I feel certain of. Everything else? I just don't know."

Tori stood and held out her hand for the empty ice cream carton. "The good news is, you don't have to decide anything tonight. Or for a while. Take your time. Pray on it."

A sob caught in Kelly's throat. "I don't deserve God. Or to be forgiven."

"Girl, none of us do."

Tori dropped the empty cartons in the trash before she came back over with a box of tissues. She handed it to Kelly and sat down again.

"Do you think Matt and I can make it through this?"

"I know you can. Especially if you turn to God."

Tori scooted closer and took Kelly's hand. "Do you want me to pray with you?"

Kelly nodded before she bowed her head. Tori offered a long prayer, asking God for wisdom. Affirming what was in Kelly's heart—regret and a desire for forgiveness. The words soothed the pain in her heart.

Even though she felt God's forgiveness, she knew the coming months—and longer—would be difficult. Her life and Matt's had changed irrevocably. Yet God promised to always be with them. That promise wasn't conditional, based on perfection. It came with grace and mercy. This child could still have a good life. So could Kelly and Matt. They just needed to rely on the One who never left them.

29

Matt

MONDAY MORNING AFTER the church staff meeting, Matt hung back, waiting for Pastor Chris to finish a conversation with a staff member. His throat tightened, and he sent up a quick prayer for the words to say.

"Matt." Pastor Chris smiled. "Don't have to rush off to work today?"

"Not today."

He cleared his throat, and his shoes scuffed the floor as he shifted from foot to foot. "I was wondering if you and Pastor Miles had a few minutes. I need to talk to you."

Pastor Chris asked him to take a seat in his office while he went to find Pastor Miles. A few minutes later, Chris brought him over to Pastor Miles's office. Bookshelves lined two walls from floor to ceiling with many thick tomes.

Matt slowly eased into the chair across from Pastor Miles, the leather creaking under the slow movement. Chris angled his chair so he could easily make eye contact with both men. After he let out a loud breath, Matt rubbed the back of his neck.

"There's no easy way to say this." Heat spread up his neck and over his face. "I have to step down."

Chris frowned as he leaned forward. "Why? What happened?"

Matt forced himself to make eye contact, even though he didn't want to. This was all his fault and he would own it. "My girlfriend is…"

After he sucked in a sharp breath, he blurted out the awful truth. "I spent the night at her house and she's pregnant."

Chris's eyes went wide as he rubbed his hands on his pants. Pastor Miles's mouth turned down as he rested his hands on the top of his desk. Pastor Miles glanced at Chris.

When Chris sputtered, Pastor Miles spoke, "I'm sorry to hear that."

"What are you going to do?" Chris asked.

Matt frowned. Through gritted teeth, he said, "Become a father."

"No, I meant… Do you think you'll marry her?"

Matt opened his mouth to answer when Pastor Miles held up his hand.

"First, thank you, Matt, for telling us. I know it took a lot of courage to come here today and to resign. We know how much you enjoyed working with the youth. Were gifted at it too."

Resign. Enjoyed.

He knew they would accept his resignation. He knew they expected it from him. Yet, the finality of Pastor Miles's words knifed his heart. He would miss working with the youth.

"How can we come alongside of you?" Miles asked.

Matt glanced out the window as he slowly exhaled.

"Right," Chris said. "How can we help you and Kelly?"

"Pray."

A knock sounded on the door and Matt pursed his lips while Pastor Miles's secretary reminded him about an appointment. He stood.

"Matt, we really appreciate everything you've done in the youth ministry. I know it seems like things are unraveling right now. God isn't finished with you yet. This is a painful lesson to be sure, but He is in the business of redeeming lives. Don't you ever forget that."

Chris asked Matt to follow him to his office to continue

their conversation.

"Will you finish seminary? You're so close."

"I... Probably not."

"Why?"

Matt snorted. "I'm disqualified from ministry now. So, what's the point?"

Chris's eyes softened. "For now. I know you, Matt. Willful disobedience isn't like you. After a time, you'll be able to work in ministry one day."

Matt refused to hope. He still wasn't sure if he wanted it. All the doubts he faced before he met Kelly resurfaced. None of it mattered. He failed. Morally failed. There was no coming back from that.

"Well, if you quit, it shouldn't take much to pick it up later if you decide you want to."

Matt nodded numbly. He stood, hoping to end the awkward, heart-rending conversation.

"Please let us know how we can help you and Kelly. You are both still part of this church family and we want to sup-port you however we can."

The kindness of Chris's words nearly undid him. He didn't deserve a thing from them. Not a prayer. Not so much as a smile. When Chris pulled him into a quick man hug, Matt swallowed the lump in his throat. He mumbled something and hurried out of the office to the safety of his car.

That was it. He was no longer in ministry. No longer helping kids meet Jesus. No longer being the male role model for teens without one.

His eyes burned, and he pinched the bridge of his nose. His shoulders slumped as he turned on his car and drove home.

Once home, Matt braced himself for the next conversation with his faculty adviser at the seminary. It went about the same. His adviser supported his decision to withdraw. He also reminded him that the credits he completed would still count toward his degree if he came back later.

After he powered off his laptop, he flopped down on his bed and stared at the ceiling.

Nothing about his life looked familiar. No more school. No degree either. Ministry—over. Now he had to decide, and soon, if he wanted to marry Kelly or not. His stomach tightened. For the first time in a very long time, escaping through a drink sounded good.

30

Kelly

ON TUESDAY AFTERNOON, Kelly glanced at her phone while she walked, the sun beaming down on her back. She went back to her office after her meeting with Chef Foley. Still nothing from Matt. They hadn't spoken since Sunday. She couldn't shake the feeling that something bad had happened.

A tear slid down her cheek. If she had known one night of desire would destroy them, she never would have asked him to stay. It was her fault. She wanted his comfort so much she didn't realize how hard it would be for him to say no to her.

Despite repenting and praying about her situation, Kelly's anxiety grew. She really liked Matt. Thought she might love him. But the silence tore at her confidence. Doubts crept in. How well did she know him? Did she want to commit to a lifetime with him?

Her purse made a loud thump as she tossed it onto her desk. Kinda late for that. Just like Kyle would always be in her life because of Alana, Matt would be, too.

Single mother of two children. The thought made her stomach churn as loneliness overwhelmed her.

If she married Matt, then their child would live in a two-parent home. But what if their marriage, starting on a rocky foundation, became unstable? What if it turned out as bad as her parents' marriage had? She knew from personal experience that divorce, and all the led up to it, was no picnic. It left scars on her heart.

Kelly sat in her office chair as it creaked beneath her. She tapped on Matt's name on her phone and stared at it.

She typed out: *Thinking about you.*

Then she deleted it.

Any plans for tonight?

Then she deleted it.

Even though it was Valentine's Day, she had no expectations for the evening. She doubted if Matt even realized it, given the upheaval in their lives.

Lord.

Words fled her mind. She sat up straighter in her chair and reached for a folder. Then set it back down.

Lord, help. I don't even know what to pray. We messed up. We gave into temptation. I... I shouldn't have asked Matt to stay. I should have done so many things differently. Please show us the way forward.

A knock sounded before the concierge entered, carrying an enormous bouquet of red roses. "These came for you."

Kelly stood and reached for the card as he placed the vase on the corner of her desk.

Happy Valentine's Day, Love, Matt.

Tears burned her eyes. He sent her flowers at work. Maybe there was hope for them yet.

After smelling the sweet scent of the roses, she reached for her phone and texted him. *Thank you.* Followed by a few heart emojis.

Meet me at my place at six?

Kelly hesitated. They shouldn't be alone.

Tori and Joe will be here to watch Alana. I have a surprise for you.

She wanted to be happy and excited. A tiny part of her heart was. Yet the tension between them still seemed palpable.

Will be there.

Ugh. She could have tried harder to sound more enthusiastic. Too late now.

A few hours later, Kelly picked up Alana and drove home to change into stylish jeans and a flowing top. Then she went to Matt's.

When Matt opened the door with a big smile and shining hazel eyes, Kelly felt the tightness release from her shoulders. The old Matt—the one she fell in love with—stood before her.

"Come on in. Alana, Tori has a surprise for you in your room."

"Yeah!"

Alana darted around him and into her bedroom.

"Now, for your surprise, Kelly. Close your eyes."

She screwed up her face, and she slouched.

Matt winked. "Trust me."

Taking a moment to relax, she slowly exhaled and closed her eyes. He took her hand and led her forward. The whoosh of the sliding glass door sounded in front of them.

"Keep them closed. Slight step down."

"Okay."

"I mean it."

The door closed with a soft thud behind them. Soft music sounded in front of her. Then Matt stood behind her and wrapped his arms around her before resting his chin on her shoulder. His warmth eased the last of her fears.

"Open them," he whispered, his breath tickling her neck.

"Oh!" she exclaimed as she took in the transformed yard. A string of Edison lights criss-crossed from a few poles. Candles cast a glow on the beautifully decorated table. A short vase of flowers added to the perfect setting.

"It's so lovely."

"I hoped you'd like it."

Then Matt twined his fingers with hers and escorted her to the romantic setting. He held her chair out for her. Once she sat, he lifted a dome cover from her plate. The aroma of garlic and rosemary made her stomach growl.

"Did you make this?" she asked as she studied the plate. Pork medallions cut to perfection and topped with a balsamic drizzle nestled against roasted potatoes seasoned with fresh garlic and rosemary. Roasted rainbow carrots completed the dish. Her mouth watered.

"I did."

Kelly smiled, her heart fluttering. All of this for her. How much time had it taken to set it up?

Matt sat across from her. His eyes glimmered in the low light as a smile stretched across his lips. "I thought you deserved a special night."

This was Matt. Kind. Caring. Serving. She loved him more for it.

"Sparkling cider?"

"Certainly."

He poured the bubbly liquid into two fluted glasses. Then he rested his hands on the table, palms up. She placed her hands in his before he prayed for the meal and for their relationship. When he finished, they began eating.

"This is so good. Where did you learn how to cook like this?"

"I worked as a line cook at a fancy restaurant in high school and college. Learned a lot about cooking there."

"You can cook for me anytime."

"Thank you."

They chatted briefly about their day. After they finished the meal, Kelly asked about church.

Matt's smile faded, and his gaze slid to a dark corner of the yard. "I resigned from the internship and working with the youth."

Kelly's heart pounded against her rib cage. "You told them?"

He nodded.

"How did it go?"

His gaze flitted back to her. "It was one of the hardest

things I've ever done. Both Pastor Miles and Pastor Chris were compassionate about it. Chris told us to let them know if there is anything they can do to help us."

She groaned. "I suppose I'll need to buy baby stuff."

"Tori said she and the girls want to host a baby shower when the time is right."

Kelly nodded. Then she propped her elbows on the table and rested her chin on her hands. The evening air chilled her arms.

"I'm sorry," Matt said. "I'm sorry I acted so irresponsibly."

Tears burned her eyes. "I'm sorry I manipulated you into staying."

"Kel, that's not true. You didn't think that would happen any more than I did."

"True." But she should have known better.

"I would like to move on from it. See if we can't focus on happier thoughts. Get to know each other better. Look forward to the birth of our… child."

"Yeah. We have to move forward. Before we know it, he or she will be here."

Matt reached across the table and squeezed her hand as he set a small box in front of her. Her throat constricted. *Please no.* She wasn't ready for a proposal.

"It's not much, but I wanted to give you something special for our first Valentine's Day."

First?

She wasn't ready to think about them as a couple for the long-term. Her hand shook as he opened the box. Then he lifted a necklace from it. The breath left her lungs on a soft whoosh as she studied the double entwined hearts with a small diamond tucked where they joined.

"This is how I feel about us, Kel. Two hearts entwined. Even though I've only known you for a short time, I love you. You are beautiful and smart. You're a great mom. And my heart is connected to yours already. You mean so much to me. I don't want to lose you."

Red rimmed his shimmery eyes before he stood and circled around behind her. He fastened the necklace for her. Then he pressed his soft lips to her cheek.

A sob escaped her mouth. Matt crouched next to her chair and looked up at her.

"What's wrong?"

"Nothing. Everything."

He held her hand between his. She touched the necklace with her other hand.

"It's beautiful. And you…"

She cupped his face in her hands, feeling the scratchy stubble.

"I don't deserve a man like you."

He stood and held her chair. Then she rose and accepted his gentle embrace. After a few seconds, he pulled back enough to study her face. Then he lowered his lips to hers for a soft kiss. All those warm, wonderful feelings ignited in her heart again. She loved this man.

31

Matt

"KYLE!" MATT CALLED after him.

"What?"

"Forgetting someone?"

"Oh. Come on Alana. It's time to go."

Matt flashed a reassuring smile at his nervous roommate.

"Are you marrying Niki today?" Alana asked, as Kyle led her to the garage.

"Yeah."

"I wish my mom would get married."

The words pierced Matt's heart. He still wasn't sure if Kelly wanted to or not. They danced around the conversation every time he tried to bring it up.

It had been five and a half weeks since Valentine's Day. Things with her settled into a routine. Unless she was working, they often ate dinner at his house. On Wednesdays, they rode together to Chad and Marcy's house for home group. The home group pastor had called and asked Matt to step down from that, too.

After the past few years of filling every spare minute on his calendar with work, home group, youth, school, and the internship, he finally settled into a quieter life. Work, dating, home group, and church on Sunday. The nights where Kelly had to work loomed large and lonely.

Once he finished picking up the house, he donned his tux for the wedding, then Joe drove them over to the venue.

Both Matt and Joe would stand with Kyle. It had surprised him when Kyle asked him to be the best man. He patted his pocket again. Yup, the rings were there.

"You clean up nice," Kelly teased as she greeted him with a kiss.

Her rose-scented perfume tickled his nose as he allowed his gaze to travel the length of her pastel floral dress. "Not bad."

She quirked an eyebrow. "That's the best you've got?"

He grinned. "You look sensational."

A giggle escaped those lovely pink lips. "That's better."

Alana called for her, bringing the ring pillow with her. Though unconventional, Kyle wanted his daughter to stand by him with the rings.

"Do you have the rings?" Kelly asked.

Matt handed them to Kelly, and she secured them to the white satin pillow.

"I'll hold on to this until right before you walk up the aisle."

Alana pouted for a second. Then she hugged Matt's waist.

As the guests arrived, Matt and Joe led them to their seats. All of Kyle's immediate and extended family came. Since Niki's parents and brother had passed a long time ago, her side would have been empty. Kyle insisted his parents sit on the bride's side, especially since the plan was for his dad to walk Niki down the aisle.

When Matt took his place in front next to Kyle, his friend moved from foot to foot.

"Breathe easy, bro," he whispered.

Kyle's back straightened, and he stilled as the music started. Matt watched Marcy, Niki's best friend, as she walked down the aisle. Then Tori followed behind before Alana brought the rings. She stood next to her dad, whose hand shook slightly as he rested it on her shoulder.

When the wedding march sounded, Matt's heart lurched

and his mouth went dry. What would it be like to be standing in the groom's place waiting for Kelly to walk toward him? His eyes scanned the seats until he found her. She glanced at him and he smiled at her. One breath. Two. At last, she smiled softly and his heart expanded in his chest.

Could they make a go of it forever?

Niki positioned herself beside Kyle while Matt concentrated on the ceremony. He listened to the vows, vows he would eagerly make to Kelly. No longer did doubt cloud his heart. He knew what he wanted. And it was her as his wife and the mother of his children. For a lifetime.

Soon, the ceremony finished. Kyle dipped his wife back, kissing her until she blushed. Then the two of them grinned and left the sanctuary. Matt escorted Marcy and Joe accompanied Tori.

After all the guests had arrived at the reception, Matt kept smiling for every wedding photo. Kelly made sure Alana's dress looked flawless, and she smiled in every shot.

"Can we get one of me and Kelly?" Matt asked.

"Of course," Kyle said. "And one with the two of you and Alana would be nice."

Matt slid his arm around Kelly's waist and held her close to his side, praying that one day soon she might be ready to say yes to a lifetime with him.

The reception and food were amazing. But his favorite part of the night was dancing with his girlfriend. During one slow dance, he braved the question pressing on his mind.

"Could you picture us doing this?"

Kelly sucked in a sharp breath. "I... I'm not sure yet."

Despite the pain pricking his heart, he rested his head against hers as he held her close and swayed to the music. Maybe when she started to show, things would seem more real, and she would be open to a proposal.

32

Kelly

KELLY BREATHED IN Matt's spicy cologne. He smelled amazing. Dancing with him felt so natural. Perfect.

When he asked if she could picture them marrying, she lied. She had envisioned the entire wedding in the few seconds her gaze had collided with his during Kyle's wedding.

As she rested her head against his shoulder, she felt the warmth of his nearness radiating against her. She loved him. That was no longer a question.

But it was too soon. She didn't want him to propose out of obligation. She wanted him to propose because he really loved her and wanted to spend his life with her. Not because she was pregnant with his child.

"Uh, oh. Somebody's getting sleepy," Matt whispered.

Kelly lifted her head and followed his gaze. "I should take her home."

"Let me walk you to your car?"

"Sure."

Matt carried a groggy Alana in his arms. Then he laid her in the back seat and eased the door closed.

Kelly leaned against the car, as had become their habit. He erased the distanced between them and kissed her softly for a few seconds. Then he ran his fingers down her cheek and neck until he lifted the entwined hearts necklace he had given her. Her skin tingled in the wake.

"I love you, Kelly. Remember that every time you wear

this. I love you so much."

"I love you too." She offered a smile.

"See you in the morning?"

She nodded before she ducked into the car.

Once back at home, with Alana in bed, Kelly propped up several pillows on her bed. She turned on the TV and flipped mindlessly through the titles on her streaming service before she turned it off.

Would it be so bad to marry Matt? He was a godly man. One mistake didn't make his character void. He still cared deeply for people. For her. For her daughter.

Lord, what should I do?

Silence.

She sighed and snuggled lower in her bed. Memories of their night together came to mind. Though she regretted not waiting until marriage, it was hard to ignore the chemistry between them. And in the almost two months since that night, they had spent a lot of time together, deliberately getting to know one another.

Kelly had opened up about the hurt over her father's fall from grace and her parents' divorce. She told him about feeling abandoned by her friends during that time and also after her ex broke up with her.

Matt shared about his family. His abusive alcoholic father. His manipulative mother. Mark, his drug-addict brother. His stepfather sounded controlling and not much better than his biological father.

Despite learning about each other's pasts, Kelly always avoided conversations about the future. At seven weeks, she still easily hid her pregnancy. Soon enough she would need maternity clothes, baby clothes, a crib, and the plethora of things the mom of a newborn needs.

As she remembered the early days with Alana, her heart ached. It had been so hard being a single mother. She didn't want to do it again. Matt would go through it with her, if only she would let him. But was she who he really wanted?

Would he grow tired of her and want someone new in ten years, like her dad had?

Her eyes burned. She knew they ought to talk about it. But if she went there, everything would feel too real. She would have to deal with her grudge against her dad, finally.

If she married Matt, would she even want her dad and, she swallowed the bile in her throat, her stepmother and half-sister to attend?

Kelly shook her head. Her life seemed as messed up as a soap opera. Maybe one day it would feel normal again.

33

Matt

MATT FOUND JOE dancing with Tori, her head tucked against his chest. They made a fine-looking couple. No way would he interrupt that. Maybe his friend finally realized the woman loved him.

Instead, he texted him and told him he was taking a ride-share home. Then he punched in the request in his app.

A few minutes later, at his house, he frowned at the sight on his front porch. Mark laid on the hard concrete, arm tucked under a scruffy cheek. Next to him was a baby in a car carrier.

"Mark!"

He nudged his brother's leg. Mark didn't move, but the baby stirred, then wailed.

Matt ran a hand through his hair. Then he opened the front door, carrying the baby inside. He shut the door behind him. Let Mark sleep it off outside. Even though it was March, after a quick check of the weather, he would be fine. Forecast was upper fifties overnight.

The baby's cries were like a stinging sensation reverberating around the room. When Matt unstrapped her from the carrier, a paper fluttered to the floor. He crouched down and picked it up. While he bounced the girl on his hip, he read the note.

Matt, I give up my parental rights for my daughter, Charity. My life is no life for a little girl. Her mother died of an overdose last week. I can't take care of her. Take her. You are the most decent person I know. She doesn't deserve to go into the system because her dad is such a loser. Your brother, Mark Dixon.

Matt swallowed hard as a lump formed in the back of his throat. This poor little girl. He was her uncle. An uncle. His hands felt numb as the implications grew more apparent.

He snorted. Ironic name, given that Mark wanted to impose on Matt's charity. It didn't really matter. Protectiveness, like he had never known, surged through him. No way would he abandon his niece.

Charity continued to wail. He didn't know if she was hungry or needed changed or what. After a quick check in the baby carrier, he found only a birth certificate. Nothing else. No diapers. No bottle.

So, he opened the front door to an empty porch, stomach sinking under the disappointment. Mark had disappeared, leaving nothing to take care of a baby.

Matt closed his eyes. That was just like Mark.

He quickly dug his phone from his pocket and dialed Kelly. Hopefully, she wasn't asleep yet. She would know what to do.

34

Kelly

"MATT?" KELLY ANSWERED her phone. The sound of a very unhappy baby screaming in the background muffled his words.

"Kel, any chance you've picked up a few baby things yet?"

"No... Why?"

"Mark. I'm an uncle. He left Charity here. There's a note and nothing else. I don't know what to do."

"He didn't bring any diapers or bottles or anything?"

"Nope."

The gravity of his single word answer caused her heart to clench in her chest.

"I can run out and get some stuff, but I'll have to wake up Alana."

"I don't think this carrier will work in my car, so I don't think I can leave. Joe is still at the reception."

"Along with everyone else I know," she said.

The cries seemed even louder in Matt's silence.

"Wait. Where's Dwight live? He's married, right?"

"Yeah. But they don't have any babies." Desperation coated each of his words.

"That's okay. Maybe his wife would come watch Alana while I go pick up some things."

A rush of air came across the earpiece. "Yeah, that's a great idea."

"I'll call you back."

Kelly hung up and dialed Dwight's number. She explained the situation and learned they only lived ten minutes away. His wife was happy to help and even had a few baby things left from when their three-year-old was born.

About fifteen minutes later, Mayra Durham showed up on her doorstep with a large box of things.

"I don't have any diapers or formula, but there's enough in here to get by for a few days."

"Thank you. Let's go up to Alana's room. I'll wake her up so she can meet you."

After the introductions, Alana fell back asleep. Kelly loaded the baby things into her car. Then she stopped at the big box store to pick up the necessities.

Once she stowed diapers, wipes, baby powder, formula, and a few other essentials in the cart, she maneuvered it to the baby aisle. A pang of longing and dread filled her as her eyes burned. She blinked rapidly to force down the emotions as a worker made a garbled announcement on the overhead speakers.

Her eyes roamed over the standard newborn things. She snagged a car seat—a must-have, so Matt would have the freedom to leave his house. Her shoulders raised, then dropped. Besides, she needed one of her own in a few months, anyway. It wouldn't hurt to buy it early so she could help Matt with Charity.

After paying for the purchases and loading them into her car, she drove to Matt's.

When he opened the door, she scooted inside with arms full of shopping bags. He looked frazzled, with his hair sticking every which way. He still wore his tux from the wedding. The bow tie hung loose, trailing down the center of his chest.

Kelly held out her arms and wiggled her fingers. "Here, let me hold her while you go change."

Matt thrust the stinky baby toward her before he spun

on his heel toward his room.

"Aren't you precious?" she asked the cranky infant.

After she ripped open a package of diapers, she tossed the old, smelly one in the trash. Then she cleaned Charity and placed the fresh diaper on. Charity calmed and started cooing, offering Kelly a happy giggle. Her hazel eyes cleared—eyes that matched her uncle's. Kelly's heart warmed as she placed the beautiful little girl in the carrier again.

When Matt returned wearing workout shorts and a fitted t-shirt, he said, "She smells better already."

"I think she's hungry, too. I'll prep some formula." She tossed him her keys. "There's a box from Mayra in my trunk and a car seat, too."

A few minutes later, she held Charity in her arms again and fed her. A flood of emotions overwhelmed her. Memories of Alana as a baby.

Moisture gathered in the corner of her eye. She would give birth in November. Reality slammed into her chest in a deeper way. She remembered the late-night feedings. The sense that time dragged on forever with no hope of peaceful sleep. Praying for the day Alana had been old enough to take her to daycare so she could go back to work, yet not wanting to leave her baby girl.

She sniffed as Matt placed his warm arm around her shoulders, a hint of his cologne comforting her. Was he looking down at his niece, wondering what it would be like to hold their newborn?

"Mark left a note. He wants me to raise her."

Kelly's head pounded as she glanced down at the baby in her arms. Wouldn't that be so much better for Charity? No longer living in squalor and danger. Raised by an imperfect yet godly man. Or parents.

Slowly, the thought wrapped its way around her heart. She could love Charity, too, as her own.

An image flashed through her mind. Matt, her, Alana,

Charity, and another baby posing for a picture at Christmastime at church. An instant family of five.

Could this be her purpose? Could this be the reason she and Matt worked hard to overcome the adversity created by their own mistakes?

Out of nowhere, peace washed over her like a gentle breeze on a spring morning. She breathed in the soothing air of the Spirit's presence. This changed everything. Suddenly, marriage didn't sound so bad.

35

Matt

MATT CLEARED HIS throat as he watched Kelly prepare the bottle and feed his niece. Something in his heart shifted. She seemed so in her element. His eyes burned. She would be a wonderful mother to their child.

As he ran a hand through his hair, he wondered how Charity's arrival would affect his relationship with Kelly, yet again. So many changes in such a short time. That old restlessness pressed against him. Desire for an escape from the crushing responsibility.

Man up, Matt. He chastised himself. He was thirty-three years old. He had a stable job. It might not be his dream job, but it paid well. More than enough to support himself and a family. His throat constricted.

Marrying Kelly came with a ready-made family. Kelly. Alana. Their baby.

He held back a snort. He came with his own little one now. Sweat dotted his forehead as his throat tightened, Charity's sweet babbling failing to improve his mood.

Slowly, Matt slid his arm away from Kelly's shoulders. Then he yanked the fridge open and poured a glass of water for both of them. The pressure weighed heavily on him. He needed to go to a meeting. Ha. Like he could just leave his niece alone at — he glanced at his watch — ten fifteen at night.

Where was Joe? He needed to talk to someone who understood the seduction of alcohol.

Not that it mattered. They didn't keep any in the house and he wasn't about to leave to go buy some. Not with a baby depending on him.

After all this time, how could the temptation be so consuming? Not a drop in thirteen years. Now, as his life rapidly spiraled out of control, it whispered its enticing lies to his soul.

Pray. He could still pray.

Lord, help me. Strengthen me. I need you. Not an escape. I need your guidance and presence and wisdom. I don't recognize my life. It's like I woke up one day and the man I thought I was — he's gone. It's too much. Way too much.

"Hey," Kelly said as she rubbed a hand on his back. "It'll be alright. We'll figure this out."

Matt hung his head in despair, and his shoulders slumped. Did she really mean she would walk through this new bombshell with him?

He turned toward her and drew her into his arms. As she rested her cheek against his neck, he drank in her presence. Comfort wrapped around him, along with her arms.

"It's too much," he whispered into her silky hair.

"It's a lot, Matt. But not more than we can face. God is with us. He promises never to leave us, never to forsake us. His timing is perfect, even... even when it doesn't seem like it to us."

He released her and took a step back while holding her upper arms loosely. "Do you really believe that?"

"It's hard to believe, but I know it's true because of the years He's proven faithful in my past."

"Why this? Why thrust my niece into my life? For me to be her provider?" He shook his head. "How can this be His purpose, His design for me?"

Kelly placed a hand on his cheek. "Matt, what kind of life would Charity have with Mark? What kind of life did she have with her mother?"

Matt didn't want to picture it. A baby in drug dens. On the street. Crying while her parents numbed the pain.

The idea hit him with such intensity that he stumbled

back, his chest pounding with each breath he took. He wanted to numb his pain, escape just like his brother. Something was seriously broken inside of him. Even after all the years of sobriety, he was still one poor decision away from a life like Mark's.

But for the grace of God. The still small Voice whispered to his soul.

"But for the grace of God," he whispered.

"Exactly," Kelly said. "God's grace is still at work in your life. And most definitely in this sweet little girl's."

"Thank you." His gaze locked with hers as he allowed the silence to calm him.

Kelly yawned. "I really ought to head home now. Do you think you can manage tonight? I'll come over tomorrow and we can set up a room for her. Buy whatever is needed. I'll help you with this."

"I don't have a crib."

The pressure climbed up his back until Kelly rested her soft hand on his forearm.

"She can sleep in the carrier. I'm sure she's used to it."

Then Matt wrapped her in his arms one more time before she left for the night. She continued to surprise him. Maybe, just maybe, she had warmed up to the idea of becoming his wife.

36

Kelly

THE NEXT MORNING, Kelly woke early. She dropped Alana off at church and asked Marcy and Chad to pick her up when the children's program finished. Marcy reassured her she looked forward to spending the day with her niece.

Even though she hated missing the service, Matt needed her help to get ready for life with a four-month-old. Once she arrived at his house, they set Charity close by in the shade while Kelly asked Matt to install the car seat into her car. She could have done it, but knew the practice would make his life easier when he installed one in his car later that day.

After his second attempt, without success, he stepped back from the car.

"Did you buy the most difficult one to install?" He wink- ed, to her relief.

"Rule number one with baby stuff: nothing is ever as easy as everyone says."

"Check."

Kelly threw her head back as she laughed. "Do you want me to try?"

"Let's take a break."

He shut her car door with a gentle thud before clasping her hand in his. Then he lifted Charity's carrier and led Kelly inside.

When Charity fussed, Kelly instinctively reached for her. Matt shook his head.

"I'll get her. I need to get used to being a single dad."

She was fully aware of the solitude single parenthood could bring, and her heart ached in response. Maybe they should get married. Then she could help more.

"Don't look so worried," he said. "I'll figure it out."

"Aren't you the glass-is-half-full this morning?"

His laughter was deep and hearty. "I'm not gonna lie. It's all overwhelming. But I'm not alone, as my wonderful girlfriend reminded me."

Kelly's phone pinged, and she glanced at the incoming message.

"Oh! Mayra and Dwight are coming over to help."

Matt's eyes widened in disbelief as he exhaled sharply. "That's good. Maybe he can help me get the car seat install-ed."

A few minutes later, the Durhams arrived with an SUV loaded with more things.

"I got so excited when I heard you had a little one. I saw this rocker at a yard sale on the way to church and made Dwight pull over."

"We were almost late to church, sweetheart, because of your haggling."

Mayra waved her hand dismissively as her eyes sparkled with restrained laughter. "It was for a good cause."

Kelly's heart warmed as she carried the glider footstool in the house while Matt and Dwight unloaded the rocker.

"We'll put it in my room for now. Kyle still needs to move his stuff, and Alana's out, but he and Niki aren't due back from their honeymoon for two weeks."

Dwight made a hissing sound as he sucked in a sharp breath between his teeth. "Not much room left in here. Maybe we should move your desk out to another room. Especially if you're gonna squeeze a crib in there."

Kelly spoke up. "We can move Alana's things to one side of her bedroom and set up the nursery in there. Or even put some of her things in Kyle's room."

"Great idea," Mayra said. "I'm assuming you'll pick up a baby monitor while you're out shopping today, so no need to rearrange your room, Matt."

Once they cleared some space in Alana's room for the nursery, Matt asked for Dwight's help with the car seat.

"Why do you want to put it in Kelly's car?"

Heat warmed her face right along with the red creeping up Matt's neck. Matt rubbed a hand on the back of his neck as his gaze dropped to his feet.

"I bought it to help. I figured Matt would want to pick out his own once he sees all the choices," she quickly explained as she wiped her palms on her soft jeans.

"Uh. Alright." Dwight said. Mayra lifted an eyebrow, but said nothing.

While Dwight and Mayra rounded to the other side of her car, Matt whispered, "Nice save."

"Yeah. Although they're gonna find out soon enough."

When Matt looked away, she noticed the fine lines around his eyes and dark circles underneath. Clearly, he hadn't slept well, despite his attempts to remain positive this morning. She understood what that was like.

"All done!" Mayra exclaimed, her hands brushing together with a soft swish. "It's just like the one we had in my SUV when Esther was little."

Kelly and Matt thanked them before they left. Then he went inside to get Charity. Once he buckled her into the newly installed car seat, he hopped in the passenger side, his khaki shorts scraping softly against her cloth seats.

"Ready?" she asked with a smile, hoping he found it encouraging.

"Thanks for helping me, Kel. I would be completely lost without you."

"Happy to help. I figured we'd do some shopping together soon, anyway."

Matt went quiet after that as she drove them to the big box store.

"I have so much to do." He ran a hand through his hair.

Kelly held his hand in hers and gave it a quick, reassuring squeeze.

"I'm not sure if Mark's note is legal or not. I suppose I'll need to figure that out. Then there's medical insurance. Daycare. And probably a thousand other things I don't know about yet."

"Breathe, Matt. One thing at a time. Can you take some time off work?"

"Yeah. It's just all too much." His mood had shifted from cheery to tense and his voice dripped with uneasiness.

"Remember the worship song with the lyrics 'this is the air I breathe?' That song got me through many of the early days with Alana. God is the air we breathe. Let His Spirit fill your lungs."

"Thanks, Kelly. You'll probably need to remind me of this a few more times today alone."

She grinned, glad to help him and to lean on her experience as a single mom.

37

Matt

THE STRAIN EASED from Matt's bunched shoulders. The Spirit was the air he breathed. Life-giving. Life-sustaining. He could sort through everything he needed to. One thing at a time, like Kelly said.

As he unclipped the carrier from the base, he wondered what Kelly thought of Charity and her sudden appearance in his life. Would this make it harder for her to want to marry him? Or would it make it easier?

He shook off the thought. He needed to concentrate on getting through today.

"How do I go shopping with a newborn?" he asked, laughing nervously.

"I'll show you."

After he retrieved a cart, Kelly nestled the car carrier securely on the edges. Huh. Who knew?

"Weekend Dad," some passerby muttered.

Matt sighed as heat climbed up his neck and over his face. If they only knew. Inexperienced and ill-equipped, he clumsily pushed the cart. The wheels defiantly squeaked against the glossy floor as Kelly walked beside him. She outlined where they would start.

"I thought we'd end with the big items. That way, we don't have to lug them all over the store."

"Good idea."

Thankfully, the store had organized a bunch of the baby stuff altogether. After they purchased more diapers and everything Kelly said were must-haves, they picked up a diaper bag, clothes, and an endless list of things.

"Is there enough room in your car for all this?" he scoffed.

"I kinda wish Kyle was around. We sure could use his truck for the furniture. We might have to make a separate trip."

Matt tightened his jaw as he paid the astronomical total.

"Customer service will hold the furniture for us. Then you and Joe can come back while I watch Charity."

"You're the best." Kelly had been a pillar of strength that he never knew he needed. Words failed to express the depth of the gratitude he felt for her help.

The afternoon flew by in a flurry of activity. Joe helped him pick up the crib, dresser-changing table, and other big items. Tori, Chad, and Marcy stopped by to help assemble the furniture, organize, and do anything that needed done.

"Mommy, is Charity Matt's baby?"

He cringed at Alana's question while he folded a load of soft baby clothes.

"You know how you are Marcy's niece because she's your daddy's sister?" Kelly asked.

Alana nodded.

"Well, Charity's daddy is Matt's brother. So she's his niece."

"So she's just visiting?"

Matt cleared his throat and glanced at Kelly.

She hurried to explain. "No. Her daddy can't take good care of her, so Matt is going to instead."

"Oh." Alana looked sad for a minute. Then she grinned. "I think she'll like Matt. He's nice."

Then she came over and hugged him. "I think you'll be a wonderful daddy."

His eyes burned. He hoped so, though he still had his doubts.

THE NEXT DAY, Matt called his boss to explain what had happened. Thankfully, he told him to take off as much time as needed to get everything settled with Charity. He also gave him the number to an adoption attorney friend.

This is the air I breathe. Thank you, Lord, for providing for me and Charity.

When he called the attorney, she cleared a time for him that day. He double-checked the diaper bag, put his niece in the car, and drove to the attorney's office.

After parking, he slung the diaper bag over his shoulder and released the carrier. The office seemed more welcoming than he had expected, complete with a play area for small children.

The receptionist greeted Matt and showed him to a conference room. He set the carrier on the table, not sure if that was rude or not. Oh, well.

"Deena Kirby," the middle-aged woman extended her hand after entering the room.

"Thanks for making time for me today," he said as he shook her offered hand.

"Of course. When I heard about your situation, it sounds more urgent than many of my other clients. So, this is your niece, Charity?"

Deena Kirby leaned over his niece and smiled. She ran her fingers over Charity's belly. Charity rewarded her with a gurgle.

"So sweet."

As she sat down, the leather chair creaked and her long nails clicked against the metal of her fancy pen. She asked, "You mentioned there's a letter from your brother?"

"Yes."

Matt retrieved it from the front pocket of the diaper bag. He smoothed out the paper and handed it, along with the birth certificate, to Ms. Kirby.

"When I came home on Saturday, he was passed out on my front porch with Charity in a carrier. By the time I got her settled inside, he took off."

Deena wrote several notes. Then she studied the letter and birth certificate.

"Hmm. This is an unusual case. The first thing we need to do is get you parental rights. I can file some paperwork with the court that will allow you to decide for her care while we work to establish your brother's intent long-term."

Matt's stomach clenched. "The letter makes it clear he wants me to be her guardian."

"Not exactly. We would need to validate the signature on this letter. Even then, this is not a legally binding document."

His throat went dry, and he jammed his fingers through his short hair. "She won't have to go into the system, will she?"

"I think we can avoid that. The letter clarifies that he intentionally left her with you. This should be enough for the judge to grant you temporary custody."

"It sounds like this won't be over soon."

"I'm afraid not. Especially if you have no way to contact your brother to sign in front of a notary."

Matt's shoulders curved downwards in a wave of disappointment. He had hoped it would be easier.

"Before you leave today, we can swab both her and you for a DNA test."

He straightened in the noisy leather chair. "But I'm her uncle."

"Of course. We submit a test for familial DNA, not a paternity test. This will show that you are related to each other, which will lend credibility to your claim, especially if we can't confirm the mother's passing or your brother's wishes."

"So, I could lose her?" He choked on the words. In a few days, he had already bonded with his sweet niece. The thought of handing her over to anyone else's care made his stomach turn.

"There is a chance. However, in situations like this, the judges often rule in favor of family members, like yourself, especially when there is a desire to raise the child."

For the next half hour, Deena outlined her plan, the next steps, and the overall process. Before he left, Deena called a judge and received a temporary custody order so Matt could arrange daycare, medical, and anything else.

All of it caused his neck muscles to tighten. It could be months or longer before he received conclusive answers and permanently became Charity's guardian.

And he still had decisions to make about Kelly and their baby.

38

Kelly

ONE AFTERNOON, Kelly sat outside on the patio by the restaurant at the resort. When the server set the reuben on rye in front of her, queasiness washed over her. She sipped on the iced green tea as her gaze roamed over the turquoise pool, glistening in the mid-April sun. Too cold still for guests to enjoy the amenity. Then her eyes darted to the shadowy mountains in the distance as her mind churned over her relationship with Matt.

She had experienced a combination of excitement and apprehension when Matt became Charity's temporary guardian. Her old fear of rejection came to the surface. Would he want another child so soon? Would he decide joint-custody would be better than being a family? Did he even want her?

As quickly as those thoughts came, Kelly tried to chase them away. Matt was a godly man, despite his mistakes. He loved people, and he loved her. She thought. He certainly kissed her like he did.

They had spent most evenings together when she didn't have to work. She helped him adjust to fatherhood. Her longing to become Charity's mother deepened.

Yet, Matt hadn't proposed. They hadn't even tried to discuss marriage or their future since Kyle and Niki's wedding almost three weeks ago.

She picked a few bites of meat from the sandwich and popped them in her mouth. She swallowed and jumped to her feet when a familiar voice called to her.

"Hey stranger!"

"Mita!" Kelly hugged her friend. "How is the little one?"

She leaned over the stroller and smiled. "Such a handsome boy."

"Elan is doing well."

"Please join me," Kelly said, motioning to the seat next to her. "I'm just finishing a late lunch."

Mita sighed as she sat down across from Kelly. "Some days I miss this place. It's so serene."

"I know. I love sitting out here on my breaks. Especially when my heart is restless."

"And is it restless today?"

Kelly exhaled slowly as a light breeze whipped a strand of hair across her face. She tucked it behind her ear.

"Yes."

She glanced down at her half-eaten sandwich as the nausea returned. She pushed the plate to the side out of her line of sight.

"You have the glow of motherhood," Mita said as she studied Kelly.

Kelly nodded slowly. "I'm about nine weeks along."

"I take it this was not happy news?"

"Not exactly. My boyfriend and I certainly hadn't planned on it. Nor did we plan for his brother to dump his five-month-old on Matt's doorstep."

Mita reached across and gripped Kelly's hand in hers.

"I see I came on just the right day. Do you have time to talk?"

Kelly glanced at her watch. She could take a longer break and still have enough time to finish up a few things before the end of her day. So, she told Mita all about her messed up life.

"I think Matt doesn't want to marry me."

"Because he didn't propose over the last few weeks while trying to adjust to being a single dad? I think you should give him some grace."

Kelly's muscles tightened, and her shoulders slumped in defeat. "You're right. I'm not being fair to him."

They talked for a few more minutes until Kelly's stomach roiled. She gave Mita a parting hug and hurried to the nearest restroom, where she threw up.

At nine weeks, she thought she might have escaped morning sickness. Seemed like her baby had different ideas. Afternoon sickness. That certainly would make her job more difficult.

As she walked past the bar, she asked the bartender for a ginger ale to take back to her office. The bartender smiled knowingly. Guess everyone had figured out her secret.

"You feeling okay?" Dwight asked when he entered her office an hour later.

"Not really."

"You should go home."

"But—"

"Take your laptop if there are things you can work on from home."

Dwight turned to leave, then he changed his mind. "I know it's not any of my business, but are you... Um..."

"Pregnant?"

Dwight's face reddened.

She nodded and glanced away.

"Matt's?"

Her gaze snapped back to his. "Of course."

"Sorry to pry. Mayra wondered when we saw you at church this last weekend. She wanted... She wondered if you need a referral for a good OB. If you do, you can text her. And she said if you need anything at all, to let her know."

Kelly looked down at her hands, shame threatening to drown her. Then she slowly lifted her head and met Dwight's gaze.

"You and Mayra would still talk to us?"

Dwight snorted. "Kelly, we haven't lived perfect lives either. We aren't about to stand in judgment. We'd much rather come alongside you and Matt to help."

A tear slid down her cheek. "You and Mayra are good people."

Dwight shook his head. "Far from it. But we've been forgiven much."

"Thank you," she whispered before he left.

Then she gathered her laptop and some paperwork before she drove home. She texted Kyle to see if he could take Alana a night early. He was happy to, especially since it was his first full weekend back after his honeymoon.

Once at home, her stomach continued to feel queasy. She texted Mayra about the doctor and mentioned she didn't feel good.

Twenty minutes later, her doorbell rang. Kelly answered it, relieved to see Mayra.

"I brought some of my favorite remedies," Mayra said as she breezed into Kelly's kitchen.

A smiled twitched at the corner of her mouth as Mayra handed her a popsicle and put a few other items in her fridge and freezer. Mayra didn't stay long, but she prayed for Kelly and Matt before she extracted a promise from Kelly to make sure she would ask for help.

Then, as quickly as Mayra breezed in, she breezed out.

Kelly texted Matt to let him know she didn't feel up to dinner. Within seconds, her phone rang.

"Hey, what's wrong?" Matt's voice came across the line, his concern clear.

She told him.

"You want Charity and me to come over and cheer you up?"

"No. Kyle's picking up Alana, so I'm gonna lay down."

The line went quiet for a few seconds.

"Kel?"

"Hmm?"

"I wish I could be there to help. I want to be there for you."

A sweet shiver ran up her back as his concern humbled her. "I know."

"Love you."

"Love you, too, Matt. Kiss Charity for me."

"Will do. Call if you need me."

Kelly disconnected the call. She needed Matt. She wanted them to be a family. To live in the same house. To come home to his handsome face every day after work.

This current arrangement wasn't what she wanted at all. Sort of together. Sort of apart. She wanted to be his wife. To help him as much as he wanted to help her. She wanted to be partners in life. Forever.

She sighed as she curled up in her bed. Maybe someday soon all of that would change.

THE NEXT WEEK, Kelly had her first OB appointment with Mayra's doctor. Her heart warmed when Matt picked her up. He grinned the entire way to the appointment.

"You seem just a tad excited," Kelly said, sarcasm dripping from her voice.

"We get to see our baby today. I've never seen an ultrasound. Or heard a baby's heartbeat."

Kelly sighed. "There is nothing like it."

Matt reached over and held her hand. His grin didn't diminish until they met with Dr. Stephanie. She took the time to answer Matt's many questions.

Kelly loved how engaged he was. Eager to be a dad to their child.

When they heard the baby's heartbeat, Matt's eyes reddened and moisture glistened in his eyes.

"Wow."

Kelly smiled as he pinched the bridge of his nose.

"Everything just got real. Really real." After he cleared his throat, he asked, "When will we find out if she's a girl or not?"

Kelly snorted. "Are you hoping for another girl?"

His face turned red, and he ran a hand across the back of his neck as his chin dipped. "Kinda."

"Not for a while yet. Another eight to ten weeks from now," Dr. Stephanie answered.

"So long?" He let out a loud breath. "Well, we've got our hands full with a five-month-old, so maybe the time will go by fast."

Kelly loved the way Matt included her, as if they were already a family. She craved it with a ferocity that surpassed the need for air.

"Oh, so this isn't your first?" Dr. Stephanie asked.

"My second pregnancy," Kelly said.

"My first," Matt said. "But I recently became my niece's guardian."

Dr. Stephanie's brows rose, but she didn't pry.

As they walked out to the car, Matt grinned again. "She seemed nice. I like her."

"Me too," Kelly said. "Though I'm sure she's still trying to figure out our complicated family dynamics."

Matt snorted. "We really ought to simplify them."

Her heart raced. "What are you saying?"

"Do you want to marry me, Kelly? Be a genuine family?"

She groaned as she slid into the passenger seat, resting her head against the back. "Yes, and no."

Matt sat behind the wheel and angled toward her. "No?"

"Do you want me to be your wife? Or just the mother of our children?"

He smiled. "Both."

When he leaned forward and kissed her, her heart still doubted if he truly wanted her as a wife.

39

Matt

MATT COULD BARELY contain his joy. He saw his baby on the ultrasound. Heard the heartbeat. He was going to be a dad.

For once, the fear and doubt that usually followed the thought didn't come. Perhaps caring for Charity healed him of that. Or God had answered his prayers.

When he brought up marriage, Kelly's answer surprised him. He thought she wanted to get married. Yet, something seemed to still be in the way between them. Should he propose anyway?

He held back a sigh as he opened the passenger door for her.

"See you later for group?" he asked as he walked her to her home.

He hated this. Leaving her or her leaving every night. He wanted her to be his wife. Living in separate houses wasn't working for him anymore. He wanted to marry her and start their life together.

But she had to be ready.

After he said his farewell, Matt drove to the daycare to pick up Charity. For some bizarre reason, he decided he ought to see if his mom was home. He didn't even know if she knew about her granddaughter.

When his mom texted back that she was at home, he drove over there.

"Matt, this is a surprise," she greeted him. "Come on..."

He knew the exact moment she realized he was holding a baby as her brows rose and her gaze fixated on the carrier in his hand.

"Who is this?"

After he entered her house, he set the carrier on the kitchen bar and lifted Charity to his chest. He would never tire of the warm feeling of holding her or her sweet baby scent.

"This is Mark's daughter, your granddaughter, Charity."

Mom blinked a few times as the words sank in. "Granddaughter?"

Matt nodded.

"Can I... Hold her?"

"Of course," he said as he eased her into his mother's arms.

"Charity," Mom whispered.

Then she turned sharp eyes on him. "Why do you have her?"

Matt sighed as he sat down at the table, the wooden chair legs scratching loudly across the tile floor.

"It's a long story." Then he told her the entire tale, including his own complicated situation with Kelly.

"Two grand babies?"

"Kelly's not due until November. But, yeah. I became an uncle overnight. Or a dad. I'm still not sure which."

When Charity fussed, Mom stood. "Do you have a bottle?"

He dug one out of the diaper bag and handed it to her.

"She's so precious."

Matt let out a long sigh, as love for his little girl overflowed his heart. He desperately needed clarity if he would be her father or her uncle. The not knowing wore on him.

"Have you heard from Mark recently?" he asked.

"No. Not for months."

"If you do, please let me know. I need him to sign some paperwork so I can officially adopt Charity."

Mom agreed as she pulled a cloth from the diaper bag. Then she patted Charity's back.

"Promise me you'll bring your girlfriend by soon or invite us over. I'd like to meet her before the wedding."

Though he hadn't mentioned a wedding, his mom knew him well enough to know one would happen sooner rather than later.

"Will do."

Then Mom lamented, "I don't want to let this sweet little one go. Please call me if you ever need someone to watch her."

Matt promised he would. Then he secured Charity in her carrier and drove home.

When he arrived home, he hadn't expected to find a moving van out front.

"Joe?" he called out as he entered the room from the garage. "What's going on?"

"I'm gonna stay with my parents until I can find a place of my own."

Matt frowned. "There's no need to do that."

Joe snorted. "Yeah, there is. I don't belong in a house full of babies, bro. Not what I signed up for."

Matt's jaw twitched as his heart sank. They had been friends and roommates for more than a decade, and Joe was just gonna sneak off with barely a word. It didn't sit right.

"Besides, it's just a matter of time before you marry Kelly and she moves in."

Once Matt put Charity in her baby swing, he helped Joe load up the van. When they had everything packed, he hugged Joe.

"Not how I pictured the two of us parting ways," Joe murmured.

"Me either. Not by a long shot."

"See you around. You know, at church and home group."

"See ya."

As Joe drove away, Matt wished he had had more warning—a chance to get used to the idea of Joe not being his roommate. For fifteen years they had been best friends. Walked through a lot of trials together. Losing him in the middle of some random afternoon hurt.

SATURDAY AFTERNOON, MATT greeted Kelly when she entered his house. That nudge in his gut reminded him how much he wanted it to be theirs.

"So, your mom wants to meet me?"

"Yeah."

"Tell me about her. And can I help with anything?"

"Wanna cut up some veggies for the salad? Everything is in the bottom drawer."

"Smells good in here."

Matt decided on a nice beef roast. He would have rather grilled chicken or steaks, but Joe took the grill and smoker with him. He would have to replace the grill soon.

"My mom's name is Courtney. My stepdad is Greg. He's... Well, you'll see."

"Ah, is that good or bad?" she asked.

"There's a reason he married someone as much of a doormat as my mom."

"Controlling?"

"You could say that."

Matt ran a hand through his hair. Then he washed his hands and grabbed a stack of plates and bowls to set the table.

"Is he abusive too?" Kelly asked as she added the veggies to the salad.

He gathered the spices for his homemade balsamic dressing. Then he measured out each into a shaker bottle with olive oil, water, and vinegar. As he shook the dressing, he finally answered.

"Best I can tell, no. He's never been physically abusive. He's just a controlling narcissist. Jealous. Reads her messages. That kind of thing."

When he set the dressing bottle down, Kelly wrapped her arms around him. "How did you ever turn out to be such a great guy?"

Matt snorted. "Says my pregnant girlfriend."

Kelly brushed a kiss on his cheek. "Says the woman who loves you."

He closed his eyes and breathed deeply of her strawberry fragrance. Then he opened them. "Thank you. I needed that."

The doorbell rang, so he spun out of her embrace and walked toward the door. Charity started fussing. He glanced over his shoulder and saw Kelly moving toward the nursery.

"Where is she?" Greg asked, without a more cordial greeting.

Matt sighed. Hopefully, the whole thing hadn't been a gigantic mistake.

His mom hugged him as Greg pushed past both of them.

"Mr. Howell," Kelly greeted him. "You must be looking for your granddaughter."

Matt held back the smile twitching at the corner of his lips. Leave it to Kelly to navigate the situation perfectly.

Greg stopped and stared at Kelly and Charity, a frown furrowed in his brow.

"Please," Mom said. "Call me Courtney and him Greg. No need to be so formal."

"Would you like to hold her?" Kelly asked Greg.

Matt turned to pull the roast from the oven as Greg sputtered. When he set the pan on the counter, he noticed Greg smiling down at Charity. Well, there was a first time for everything.

Kelly hugged Mom, making him breathe easier. He figured Mom and Kelly would get along. Still, it was a relief to see it in action.

Matt poured beverages for everyone while the roast rested. Then he sliced it and set the rest of the food on the table. When he bowed his head to offer a blessing, Greg grumbled.

"None of that religious stuff."

Kelly smiled at Greg. "This is Matt's house, so his rules apply."

Greg scowled at Kelly as she bowed her head. Matt offered a quick prayer out loud. His silent one had more to do with calming his stepdad down.

Kelly offered Greg the first pick from the platter of meat, winning her additional points. She was amazing. Seemed to calm down his stepdad without letting him walk all over them.

As the conversation flowed, Matt relaxed.

"So, we have another grandchild on the way?" Greg asked.

Matt's stomach twisted in knots as he glanced at Kelly. Maybe he should have waited until after they were married to introduce her to his parents.

40

Matt

MATT'S FACE HEATED. He shouldn't be embarrassed. It's not like Greg or his mom cared that Matt and Kelly weren't married. They would never understand his perspective.

When Kelly squeezed his hand under the table, Matt nodded.

"Yes. We're having a baby."

"Due in November," Kelly added nonchalantly.

"You living together?"

Matt's spine pricked at the invasive question.

"Greg, honey —"

"I raised him better than that."

Matt's stomach churned. Greg might not have struck him, but he had done plenty to contribute to the dysfunction of Matt's teen years.

"I always told him if he got a girl pregnant, he had better marry her."

"We're still discussing our options," Matt finally said through clenched teeth.

Greg stood even though Mom still picked at her plate. "Going out for a smoke."

Then he stormed out the front door.

Kelly turned wide eyes in his direction.

"Sorry. He's obviously disappointed in me." Matt pushed his food around on his plate, his appetite gone.

Kelly snorted. Then she stood and retrieved the iced tea pitcher from the fridge.

"Courtney, would you care for more iced tea?" She refilled Mom's glass without waiting for her response.

The front door opened and then slammed shut, rattling the windows. Greg stalked toward his vacated chair and sat down again, expelling a loud huff.

Matt pushed his plate away. This had been a terrible idea. No way Kelly would want to marry him after meeting Greg. He hadn't thought that through.

As soon as Mom finished her food, Matt launched to his feet and cleared away the dishes. The silverware clanked against the porcelain plates as he stacked them on top of each other.

"Let me help," Kelly said as she followed him, balancing several serving dishes in her arms.

"Piece of work," she muttered.

"Yeah. That's Greg."

"Should I dish up dessert?"

Matt nodded. The sooner they finished, the sooner the horrible day would be over.

Once they sat around the table with the chocolate cake, Mom glanced awkwardly at Greg.

"We, um, heard from Mark."

Matt straightened in his chair, his heart thrumming against his rib cage.

"The reprobate is in prison," Greg said.

"Prison?" Matt asked.

Mom explained they had arrested Mark for possession with the intent to distribute. He was in the prison in Florence for at least a year. Maybe more.

Matt's ears rang as his vision narrowed. He could get Mark to sign the paperwork. Charity could really be his soon.

The conversation continued in fits and spurts for another half hour before Greg announced they had to go. Matt didn't mind. He was more than ready for them to leave his house.

When he closed the door behind him, he sagged against it for a minute.

"That was enlightening," Kelly said as she held out her hands for his.

"Yeah. If I didn't mention this before, I'm not really close to my parents."

"I can see why."

Then she drew him into her arms. He rested his chin on her shoulder.

"You were amazing, though. Put him in his place without provoking him too much. Then smoothing it over."

"I work in the hospitality industry, remember?" She laughed. "Did you see his face when I offered for him to hold Charity? He looked like he wanted to run away."

Matt let out a soft laugh as his body relaxed. "That was smooth. I still can't believe he actually held her for a few minutes."

"Are you going to contact your attorney about Mark?"

"Yeah, first thing Monday morning."

ON WEDNESDAY AFTER dropping Charity off at daycare, Matt rode with Deena Kirby down to the Florence prison. During the entire drive, his leg bobbed up and down. He drummed his fingers on the passenger arm rest until Deena played smooth jazz in the background.

"We shouldn't be there long," she said. "His attorney will meet us there. Then, after we're through security, it should be a quick meeting."

"Unless he changes his mind." Matt's jaw tensed with the thought.

"Do you think he will?"

Reason told him no, but doubt kept him from answering the question.

Kelly texted. *Praying for you.*

He sucked in a loud breath. Then he let it out slowly. *Lord, thank you for this opportunity to talk to Mark. I love that little girl, but I want Your Will in this. Not my own.*

Peace enveloped him like a warm hug. Everything would turn out alright. He finally understood that.

After the security guard led them into a room with a table, Matt sat down next to Deena. The cold metal table caused him to shiver. The sterile gray walls and flickering fluorescent lights added to the eerie feeling creeping up his spine.

When the guard opened the door for Mark, Matt's jaw tightened. He had lost more weight. But his eyes were clear, something Matt hadn't seen in a very long time.

The guard unlocked Mark's shackles and stood in the corner while Mark eased into the metal chair next to his attorney. The scraping of the metal legs against the hard concrete floor echoed loudly in the suffocating room.

"Matt." His brother's voice trembled, and his hands shook until he rested them flat on the tabletop.

"Mark."

Matt studied his brother for a few seconds, trying to decide what he ought to say. At last, Mark spoke, his voice still scratchy.

"Where's Charity?"

"At daycare."

Mark's shoulders fell. "Oh."

Deena slid the paperwork across the table to Mark's attorney, resting her fancy pen on top. She explained it was for Mark to give up his parental rights.

"This will enable Matt to adopt Charity and become her official guardian," she said.

"Can I... Can I still see her?"

Matt frowned and crossed his arms over his chest. His pulse raced.

"That would be up to Matt."

"You'll be her dad." Mark's voice quavered. "Can I be

her uncle?"

"If you stay clean..." Matt cleared his throat and unfolded his arms. "Then probably."

Mark's gaze slid to the paperwork. He snatched the pen up and signed quickly. Then he dropped the pen, which clattered as it rolled across the metal table.

Matt's eyes burned when he noticed a tear in the corner of Mark's eye. For all his faults, he really cared that Charity would have a suitable home.

"You'll be a wonderful dad." Then Mark nodded to the guard. "I'm ready."

Matt swallowed the lump in his throat. He didn't want those to be the last words between them for a while.

"I'll write to you about her."

Mark glanced over his shoulder. "Don't bother. I'm not worth the time. When I get out, I'll let you know."

"Mark," Matt's voice softened. "You are worth it. I'll write. I promise."

Mark shuffled through the open door, hands shackled together, as Matt's stomach clenched.

"But for the grace of God," he whispered. That could have been him on the other side of the table. If not for God rescuing him in college. If not for God's continued grace and mercy.

Deena sighed. "Amen."

When they arrived back at the office, Deena had Matt sign the official paperwork to adopt Charity.

"As soon as it's accepted by the court, I'll send you a copy."

"And when I get married, my wife can adopt her too, right?"

"Of course. Let me know when and I'll take care of it."

"Thanks for your help."

On the drive home, Matt decided it was finally time to move forward. Propose to and marry Kelly. Ready the nursery for Grace Joy. He really hoped their baby was a girl.

41

Kelly

"HOW DID IT go?" Kelly asked as she entered Matt's house after work.

"He signed."

Kelly pulled him close for a hug, knowing how hard it must have been.

"Deena is filing the paperwork with the court. Charity will be my daughter soon enough."

She smiled, but it faded quickly. She really wanted to be Charity's mom. But they hadn't talked about marriage for a while. She wondered if Matt would ever ask. Or if he really just wanted to keep things as they were.

"There's something I've been meaning to give you, but you're not gonna like it."

In two seconds, her heart rose to hope and plummeted to fear. Matt picked up a folded piece of paper from the counter and handed it to her. She tilted her head and quirked an eyebrow.

"When you were in the hospital, your dad gave me this to give to you."

Kelly's hand shook as her fingers pressed down on the edge of the paper. As the wheezing constricted her throat, she appreciated he had waited until Friday evening when Alana was at her dad's.

"Deep breath."

She took one. Then another.

"If we're going to have a wedding soon, I figure it is

time for you to repair things with your dad."

Kelly frowned, not sure which statement to latch onto. "Are we going to have a wedding soon?"

Matt winked at her. "Probably."

She walked over to the couch and flopped down on it. She propped her elbows on her knees and rested her head in her palms.

"I know you mean well, but you don't know what you're asking."

Matt snorted. "Sure I do. You met Greg. Your dad is far better than him."

Kelly stared at the number. Years of bitterness weighed her heart down. She bit the inside of her lip as her pulse raced. Matt sat next to her and looped his arm around her shoulders.

"I know you're hurt. But he showed up at the hospital that day. And he wants to meet Alana. I think he'll want to know he has another grandchild to look forward to."

"I haven't even told Mom yet."

"Why not?"

She sniffed. She had hoped to share the news of a wedding first to mask her shame of having another child outside of marriage. Matt wouldn't understand. It's not like he had made the same mistake twice.

"Kel?"

When she shifted to look at him, she tucked one leg up on the couch between them.

"This is not my first mistake, Matt. I've had that tough conversation once before. I'm not eager to have it again."

As his features softened, her heart melted. Maybe he understood better than she thought.

"Well, just think about it."

Then Matt grinned. "Let's go out for dinner tonight."

He stood and helped her up. Then he brought Charity into the room while Kelly double-checked the diaper bag. She sighed. In another six months, they would need twice as much of everything.

They made a good team, though. The last month made it obvious.

So what was he waiting for?

Kelly shook off the thought as she set the diaper bag in the back seat while Matt snapped Charity's carrier into place.

"I hope you don't mind going out tomorrow night, too."

"Oh?"

"Tori is gonna watch Charity tomorrow, so you and I can have an actual date. We haven't really had a normal date in a long time."

Her annoyance faded. Maybe he really wanted her after all. Dare she hope?

"I'd like that."

Matt flashed her a grin.

Once they arrived at the restaurant, Kelly nearly stopped breathing when her eyes snagged on her dad, his wife, and daughter standing in the lobby.

"Kelly?" her dad's incredulous tone matched his amiable smile — one she hadn't seen in a decade.

Too late to run away now. She frowned when her dad approached them. She glowered at Matt as her throat constricted.

"Did you know he would be here?" she hissed through clenched teeth.

"No. Do you want to go somewhere else?"

She sighed. "We're here. Might as well get this over with."

Then she pasted on a fake smile. "Dad."

When his gaze darted to Charity, he quirked an eyebrow.

"This is Diana, my wife," he introduced her. "And Audra, your sister."

The word stung and started a knot between Kelly's shoulder blades.

"Half. Half-sister."

Her dad dipped his head in deference.

Kelly reined in her anger. The poor girl didn't deserve it. Just Dad.

"Hi, Audra. I'm Kelly," she said in a pleasant tone as she turned her attention to the young girl.

Audra launched herself at Kelly's waist and squeezed tight. "I've waited so long to meet you."

A lump formed in her throat as Audra's joy caught her off guard. She swallowed it down.

"Very nice to meet you," she said as she rested a hand on Audra's shoulder.

Diana gave her a hug too, before she asked, "Who's this?"

"My daughter, Charity," Matt said. "It's a long story."

"Let me see if we can get them to seat us at a table together," Diana said before Kelly could stop her.

"Awkward," she muttered.

"Deep breaths," Matt whispered near her ear. "I think we should go with it. It's just dinner."

Kelly held back a growl. It was just dinner with her estranged father and the woman he had an affair with. Their love child. And her boyfriend, aka baby daddy. And Matt's niece, now his daughter. Nothing normal about any of that. At least Alana was with her dad.

Matt grinned as he placed a hand on the small of Kelly's back and kept her from running out the door. Okay, he was ushering her to the table, but it had that effect. Kelly sat across from Diana, forcing Matt to sit across from her father.

"So, that long story?" Diana prompted.

Matt launched into the tale.

"Wow. When will you know for sure?" her dad asked.

"The attorney thinks we should have the final paperwork in a few weeks. Then I guess I'll officially be a single dad."

"Oh? You're not together?" Diana asked.

Matt glanced at Kelly and winked. "Not yet."

Again, her heart fluttered at his vague hints as her face heated.

Kelly wished she could run and hide instead of going through that dinner. Yet, Matt and Diana's questions set her at ease. Matt asked her dad a few questions. Turns out he worked at their church as the new home groups pastor. Go figure. Diana was an accountant.

"Do you like Arizona?" Kelly asked Audra, trying to make sure the girl didn't feel like any of Kelly's animosity had been directed toward her.

"It's nice. All my friends at school say it gets insanely hot in the summer."

Matt laughed. "It does. Kelly hasn't been through a summer yet either."

"We have a pool, so I can't wait until Mom says it's warm enough to go swimming."

"That sounds like fun," Kelly said, not thinking anything would come of it.

"You should come over."

Kelly's eyes locked with her dad's and she narrowed her eyes.

He cleared his throat. "We'd really like to have the three of you and Alana over some time."

Her mother's voice rang in her mind. *Seventy times seven.*

Kelly's shoulders rose and fell with her exaggerated breath. "That would be nice."

She wasn't sure if she believed herself. But maybe it was time to let go of the past hurt. Diana seemed nice. Audra was only four years older than Alana. The two would get along nicely, even if Audra was technically Alana's aunt. Yeah, she didn't linger on that uncomfortable thought for too long.

"Alana is usually with her dad on the weekends, but I'm sure he would make an exception."

"Or he and his wife could come too," Diana said.

Kelly wondered how she knew Kyle was married.

"A real pool party!" Audra exclaimed, her dark eyes gleaming with excitement.

"Sounds nice," Matt said as he rubbed circles on Kelly's back.

She let out a soft breath. "Yeah."

When the server came with the check, Matt offered to pick it up.

"Let me," her dad said. "Save your money for the little one."

Kelly's breath lodged in her throat until she realized he meant Charity. No way he could tell Kelly was pregnant. Her flowing top covered her stomach. She hoped.

Diana asked to exchange phone numbers to arrange the pool party. Kelly begrudgingly handed her phone over and let Diana key in her number. Her dad's too.

When they were all outside the restaurant, Dad pulled her aside.

"Thanks for having dinner with us. And for... being so kind to Audra. She's wanted to meet you for a long time."

Kelly frowned and failed to keep the sharpness from her voice. "I can't believe you told her about me."

"Why wouldn't we? You're my daughter. I love you, sweetheart."

Kelly's eyes burned and she allowed him to hug her before they left. She practically jogged toward the car, trying to push down the flood of emotions. She didn't want to deal with them right then.

"That wasn't so bad, was it?" Matt asked as he held the car door open.

She exhaled loudly, and her shoulders drooped. "I suppose not. Did you know they would be there?"

Matt shook his head. "Promise, I did not know. But I'm glad we stayed and got to know them."

"Yeah. I guess."

When they arrived at his place, she drove home to think

about all that had happened. Maybe it had been God's way of nudging her. And it had gone better than she expected. She might even tell her dad about the mystery wedding Matt kept hinting about. If he ever proposed.

42

Matt

"YOU LOOK NICE," Tori said when Matt opened the door to his house on Saturday night.

He stepped aside to allow her in. Then he gave her a rundown of where to find Charity's things. He thanked her before he took off to pick up Kelly.

Tonight was it. He resisted the urge to run a hand through his hair. He didn't want it mussed. Not for such a special night.

When his phone buzzed, he glanced at the text. Dwight came through, after all. Just in time.

Matt rang the doorbell and waited for Kelly to open it. Nearly a minute passed, so he rang it again.

When she opened the door, his eyes widened. She had pulled her hair back in a sloppy ponytail. She wore her pjs. Dark circles rested under her eyes.

"Matt." His name came out more like a moan.

Leaving the door wide open, she ran to the bathroom. He sighed. Looks like the special night he had planned would not happen.

He heard her retching, followed by a muffled, "Sorry!"

Matt turned and locked the door before he followed her. Then he stood in the bathroom doorway as he tried to push down his frustration. His annoyance would do little to save the night or help his girlfriend.

Kelly leaned against the wall, tears streaming down her mottled face. His heart broke. She looked so miserable.

"I'm." She hiccupped. "Sorry."

"It's alright. Can I get you anything?"

She started to speak, but turned and retched again.

Matt fished his phone from his pocket and texted Dwight. *It's a no-go. She's sick.*

It figured. The night he finally planned to propose and the woman of his dreams got sick. Matt grabbed a glass and filled it with water. Then he took it in to Kelly.

"Thank you."

She sipped the water. Then she leaned back against the wall. Matt sat on the edge of the tub and studied her.

"Flu?"

She shook her head. "Baby."

"Huh?"

"Morning sickness."

That made no sense to him. "But it's six in the evening."

She snorted. Then she lifted a finger as she hung her head over the toilet again. He held her hair out of the way as disappointment washed over him.

"It's not always in the morning," she said when she composed herself again.

"Oh."

Kelly sipped the water. Then she offered a half-smile.

"You look really nice."

"Thanks."

Then she took a deep breath and handed him the glass. She held out a hand, and he helped her up.

"Okay. I think I'm good now."

Matt blinked. "You still want to go out?"

She nodded. "Yup. I think I'm good."

He frowned. He was about to tell her to forget it when she spoke again.

"Give me a minute, and I'll go change."

"Are you sure?"

The last thing he wanted was for her to get sick in the car or at the restaurant.

"Yeah. Fifteen minutes. That's all I need."

He raised an eyebrow and took a seat at the bar when she hurried upstairs. While he waited, he texted Dwight. *It's back on. I think.*

Dwight called. "What do you mean, you think?"

"She was having morning sickness. At night. I don't get it, but she says she's fine now."

"Matt?" Kelly's voice sounded in the distance from her room.

"Hang on. I'll call you back in a minute."

"Kelly?" He called her name from the foot of the stairs.

She moaned. "I was wrong."

He ran his hand through his hair. Yeah, it was off. No proposal tonight.

"I don't think I can make it."

"It's fine, Kel. We'll go out some other time."

Hopefully, he didn't sound as perturbed as he felt.

He called Dwight back. "It's definitely a no-go now."

"Sorry to hear that, bro. Anything Mayra or I can do?"

"No. I'll let you know when we can reschedule."

Only he didn't really want to reschedule the most important night of his life. He planned everything perfectly for her. She would have felt so special. He didn't think he could pull it off a second time.

Matt trudged up the stairs to check on her. His heart squeezed tight when he found her on the floor, hunched over the toilet.

"Do you want some soup or something?" he asked.

"Mmm. Chicken noodle soup sounds good. And dill pickles."

His stomach lurched. No wonder she was sick.

"And chocolate chip cookie dough ice cream."

Matt snorted. "Anything else?"

Kelly shook her head.

"Leave the door unlocked so you can get back in."

He nodded and tromped down the stairs and out to his

car. Then he drove to the grocery store for dill pickles, chocolate chip cookie dough ice cream, and chicken noodle soup. That had to be the weirdest combination of food he had ever purchased.

When his phone pinged, he glanced at it. Then he stepped out of the line and went back for some tuna salad. Shaking his head, he finally made it back to the self-checkout. Then he stopped at McDonald's for a burger meal for himself.

It was hard not to feel dejected. This was supposed to be the night he proposed to Kelly. The next step in their future together.

When he parked at her place, he tapped on the picture Dwight sent him. A perfectly set table overlooking the lit pool at the resort. Though the five-star restaurant was closed for the season, Dwight suggested he could let them eat up there as long as they didn't tell a bunch of people.

The sun eased toward the horizon in the background. Matt was going to get down on one knee and recite all the wonderful feelings and thoughts of Kelly, the woman he wanted to spend the rest of his life loving.

Instead, he carried grocery bags full of bizarre food into her townhome. Yeah, worst proposal night ever.

43

Kelly

KELLY HURRIED TO wash her face and put on something presentable. When Mayra had texted her the picture of the restaurant at the resort, she nearly cried. Matt was going to propose, and she had ruined it all. She stared at the picture again. It was perfect. Romantic. Special. No one else would ever get to sit at that table at the end of April and have the man of her dreams confess his undying love.

She sighed when she heard the door open.

A t-shirt, yoga pants, and messy hair. Not exactly how she envisioned the evening. She doubted he would go through with it that night. Not with the way she ruined everything.

Oh well. Their baby had other ideas for the night.

The cravings had started that morning. Intense and just strange. Very different from when she carried Alana. She had had some cravings, but chicken noodle soup *and* dill pickles? It sounded perfect on one level and totally gross on another. Hopefully, her food choices didn't have Matt retching by the end of the night.

"Kelly!"

"Coming!"

She padded down the stairs. When she saw the McDonald's bag, she suddenly didn't want any of the food she asked for. She swiped it from his hands and stuffed a fry in her mouth.

"Oh, my gosh. This is exactly what I wanted."

When his eyes rounded, she snickered. "Sorry. This is what cravings can be like."

He sighed. "Guess I'll put this stuff in the fridge."

"What are you going to eat?" She grimaced.

"Mind if I order a pizza?"

"Oh, that sounds good, too."

When he narrowed his eyes at her, she cringed. "I promise I'll let you eat some first. You better order a large and whatever toppings you like."

As his shoulders sagged, he tapped a few times on his phone until he finished ordering the pizza.

"Wanna fry?" She held it out to him.

When he opened his mouth, she tossed it in. He chewed it and eyed her warily.

"Thanks. How's my Big Mac?"

"So good."

He snorted and crossed his arms over his chest.

Kelly felt terrible. Well, only a little. The burger and fries were delicious. She still wanted the cookie dough ice cream. That would be dessert.

She set the burger and fries down. Then she leaned closer to Matt. His warm arms wrapped around her and she snuggled against his tailored blue shirt.

"I'm really sorry. I know you had something amazing planned."

As she pushed back, she noticed the deep creases in his brow, and she rushed to explain.

"Mayra sent me this." She turned the phone toward him.

He groaned. "Yeah, Kel. I had a really special night planned for you."

"I can see that. You even have twelve red roses on the table. It looks so perfect."

He let out a long breath. "It would have been."

A giggle bubbled up and escaped. "Surprise! Your daughter or son asserted herself."

Matt shook his head and tugged her toward him again.

When she rested her head against his neck, he stroked her hair.

"I planned an impressive speech, too."

Kelly leaned back. "Yeah? I'd still like to hear it."

"Are you sure? You want this to happen this way?"

She giggled again. "Why not? No one else will ever have our story, Matt. This is us."

He straightened and stepped around her. Then he took her hands in his.

"Just remember, you asked for this."

She winked at him and popped another fry into her mouth.

Matt tossed his head back and chuckled deeply, his voice echoing in the still house.

"Here it goes. Kelly Sutton, from the moment I pulled you up off your kitchen floor—"

"That was *not* part of your speech!"

"Maybe it was and maybe it wasn't. But it is now."

"Fine. Continue."

"From the moment I picked you up off your kitchen floor, I haven't been able to catch my breath. I love everything about you. Your smile. Your gorgeous unicorn and rainbows pjs."

He cleared his throat.

"Thanks for changing into yoga pants. That's so much better."

She laughed, her cheeks heating with the intensity of his gaze.

"Anyway, I love what a wonderful mother you are. And how you always know how to cheer me up. You defend me with my controlling stepdad. You've helped me with my daughter. Taught me how to care for her."

She smiled when his eyes reddened. Her Matt was a softy in shining armor. And she loved him for it.

"You have truly turned my world upside down and I wouldn't trade my new life for anything, save one thing."

Kelly gasped when he finally dropped to one knee in front of her. Her pulse raced as he took the fry out of her hand and placed a ring on the tip of her left ring finger.

"I want you to be my wife. To walk through life with me. To raise our odd blended family. I love you so much, Kel. Will you marry me?"

She swallowed the fry that almost lodged in her throat.

"Yes! Yes!" She jumped up and down.

As he started to slide the ring on her finger, the doorbell rang.

He laughed and shook his head as he stood.

"Guess the pizza is here."

After he set the pizza on the counter, he placed the ring on her finger.

"Where were we?" he asked.

Kelly pressed against him and ran her fingers through the hair at his nape.

"I think you were about to kiss your fiancée."

"Oh, yeah."

Then Matt kissed her until she could barely stand, her heart overflowing with love for her amazing man.

44

Kelly

THE LAST SATURDAY in May. Her wedding day.

Kelly rested her hand on her baby bump. Visible but not so big that she would look like a pregnant bride in her princess cut dress. Not that it really mattered. She was marrying Matt today. She would deliver their baby in November, completing their yours, mine, and ours—all in the wrong order.

As much as her life turned out differently than she planned, she didn't regret it. She and Matt made some mistakes. Yet, they took their time to consider whether to marry. She could hardly wait to start their life together. No more leaving at the end of the evening.

Their friends helped move her stuff into Matt's house—their house now—earlier that morning.

"You look gorgeous," Tori said as she straightened Kelly's veil.

"Thanks."

"You ready for your dad?" Marcy asked.

"I think so."

Since their surprise dinner with her dad, she had spent one other weekend evening with them. Matt, Alana, and Charity had been there, too. In time, Kelly knew it would feel less awkward. While hoping for that day, she decided she wanted Dad to walk her down the aisle, anyway.

Dad coughed as he closed the door behind him. When he leaned in, she realized she had missed him much more than she had admitted. It felt so right to share this moment with him.

"You're radiant. Matt is one lucky guy."

"Thanks. He showed, right?"

"Of course, sweetheart. He's only gotten teary-eyed once."

Kelly laughed. Then she placed her hand in the crook of her father's arm. When they made it to the back of the venue, she grinned. It was truly the happiest day of her life. Even better than when Alana was born.

Tori walked up the aisle and took her place at the front. Then the wedding march sounded, the piano music echoing in the hall.

Kelly's gaze remained fixed on Matt's red-rimmed hazel eyes the entire way up the aisle. He coughed to hide a near sob. Yeah, he loved her as much as she loved him.

When they stopped, her mother stood next to her father to give her away before they faded into the background. Kelly recited the words Pastor Chris said, never looking away from Matt. Matt blinked rapidly, and his voice was thick with emotion as he recited his vows to her. Before she could blink, he leaned forward and rested his hand on the small of her back. Then he dipped her back slightly for a world-spinning kiss.

When he righted her, he whispered, "He is the air I breathe and I'm thankful He gave me you."

That was the moment her eyes burned. Oh, how she loved this man! And would for the rest of her days.

Epilogue

Matt

"MATT!"

He rolled over, his heart pulsating against his chest as an elbow jabbed him in his back.

"Matt! It's time."

His heart jump-started as he threw back the covers.

"Now?"

Kelly panted loudly. "Now!"

"Um…"

He glanced at the clock. Two in the morning. He snorted. Of course.

Kelly's groan cleared the fog in his brain. He threw on a pair of workout shorts and a t-shirt.

"Mommy?" Alana's voice came from the doorway.

"Grab your sister," Kelly said before groaning loudly.

"I'll get her. Alana, can you take this bag to the car? Then put on some clothes?" he asked her. "Er… Get dressed first, I mean."

She took the bag and bounded out of the room.

"Come on, Kel."

She gripped his arm like a vise. As soon as Kelly and Alana were in the car, he went back for Charity. Kelly groaned. A lot. Finally, he had his ladies ready to go.

He punched his mom's phone number to ring her while he backed out of the garage.

"Ow!" Kelly groaned as his mom picked up.

"It's time, Mom. Meet us at the hospital?"

"Yeah, we'll be there."

Matt hung up at Kelly's glare.

"We?"

"I'm sure she meant her. I can't see Greg coming. Can you dial your dad?"

When her eyes speared him, he asked his smart phone to dial Brent Sutton.

"It's time," he said as he parked the car at the hospital drop off.

He hung up the phone and helped Kelly inside. His heart hammered so hard he thought he could hear it. Then he parked the car close by before he brought Charity, Alana, and several bags' worth of stuff back in.

Reality hit him square in the chest when he saw Kelly being wheeled away on a gurney. Grace Joy was on her way. His wife was giving birth.

He swayed and gripped the wall as lightheadedness hit him hard. His stomach soured as the image of his wife on a gurney played over again.

"Sir, are you alright?"

"Matt!" Brent called his name. "I've got the girls. You go."

In a weird, hazy blur, he was at Kelly's side. She squeezed his hand so tight. That was going to leave a mark.

Then a baby's cry. Matt wasn't sure how long they had been in the delivery room. None of it mattered. The moment Grace Joy Dixon rested in her mother's arms, Matt breathed again. His baby girl. His wife.

A thousand thoughts and images rushed through his mind. Every unfulfilled dream vanished. Suddenly, it didn't matter that he never became a youth pastor. He was a dad. A dad of the sweetest red-faced baby on the planet. This was the dream he hadn't known he wanted until right then. Kelly and their girls. Alana, Charity, and Grace.

"Grace," he whispered her name in awe of the little human, so small and fragile.

"She's so perfect," Kelly cried.

Her name meant everything to both him and Kelly. God granted them grace after their mistakes. He brought them unbelievable joy as a family. Matt had everything he could ever want right there.

Thank you, Lord. Help us continue to breathe in Your love and grace. Thank you for this beautiful family. May we serve You and teach our girls to love You.

"Amen," Kelly said, and he realized he had spoken the prayer aloud.

His purpose in life was to lead and provide for his family, he thought as peace enveloped him.

Bonus Epilogue

Joe

(March at Kyle & Niki's Reception)

"YOU MAKE A lovely couple," some relative of Kyle's said as Joe led Tori toward the dance floor.

The tightness in Joe's throat increased each time someone expressed a similar sentiment. He chanced a glance at Tori and noticed her quickly mask her hope. This was why he didn't want to stand for Kyle. He knew they would pair him up with Tori.

Joe had noticed her affections, contrary to what his friends believed. He knew of her fondness—maybe even love —for him.

Unfortunately, her feelings would be better directed toward someone who wanted to get married. Someone other than Joe.

Well, that wasn't entirely true. Joe would love to get married. He just didn't deserve that kind of happiness. A man with such a secret could never marry, no matter how much he liked a woman. He would be a bachelor until the day he died. That was the sentence for his sins.

As the music started, he tried to swallow back the decade old guilt. He and Tori were friends. They could never be more. Perhaps dancing with her was foolishness. No matter his resolve, he cared deeply for her. After this dance, he would let her go. He would distance himself from her for her own good.

His heart thrummed in his chest as he led her onto the dance floor. They were opposites. She was light and goodness and happiness in human form. He was dark-skinned and guilt-ridden and forever seeking to make up for his past, causing him to appear reserved to outsiders. As much as he wished to claim her for himself, he never could.

Tori faced him, and instead of taking his hand, she wrapped her arms behind his neck. Joe sucked in a sharp breath. Big mistake as the tantalizing fragrance she wore suddenly filled his nostrils, heightening his awareness of her. The bridesmaid dress hugged her curves perfectly and felt silky under his hand at her waist. She had piled her long brown hair high on her head with a few strands trailing down her back, leaving her delicate neck exposed.

Joe's mouth went dry as he wondered what it would be like to kiss her neck. He forced his eyes away from it and to Tori's. Also, a bad idea. Her eyes were full of adoration and her expression revealed it all. He couldn't look away to save his life.

He rested his hands on her waist and she snuggled against him as they swayed to the music. The moment was perfect. The night was perfect.

Too bad it could never be more. Even if he could break free of the penance required of him, her look of adoration would morph into one of horror when she learned his secret.

No, after tonight, he would do the honorable thing and let Tori go. Eventually, she would find happiness in the arms of another man.

Why did that thought bother him so much?

Continue Joe and Tori's story in: *The Shadow I Hide*

Dear Reader

THANK YOU SO much for reading. I'm honored that you chose to spend the last few hours with Kelly, Matt, and me.

As an independent author, I rely on readers like you to help spread the word about stories you enjoy. Would you take a minute to let your friends know on Facebook, Twitter, Instagram, Goodreads, or wherever you hang out online?

Also, each honest review helps readers know if this book is one they might enjoy. I would appreciate your help posting your review with online retailers.

I love hearing from readers. Stay in touch and get a free gift from me when you subscribe to my newsletter. Just go to my website and sign up at the bottom of the home page. You can also visit my website at www.karenbaney.com, email me, read my blog, and find me on many social media platforms.

Thank you so much for your support.

Karen Baney

Will Matt's dream of becoming a youth pastor finally come true?

Sign up for my newsletter and get the bonus 2 chapter epilogue for free!

https://BookHip.com/PADFVSH

Books By Karen Baney

Contemporary Romance

Vargas Ranch Series:
Love is in the air at the Vargas Guest Ranch & Resort near Wickenburg, Arizona. The Vargas family lives and breathes their family motto: *We do not deviate from the Lord's plan.* Five brawny brothers keep the ranch and resort running while life lassos their hearts in this epic contemporary cowboy romance series.

Falling for a Real Cowboy | (A, E, P)
Falling for a Shy Cowboy | (A, E, P)
Falling for a Bossy Cowboy – coming 2024
Falling for a Smart Cowboy – coming 2024
Falling for a Grumpy Cowboy – coming 2024

Steadfast Love Series:
A group of friends learn to rely on God's steadfast love as they navigate life's ups and downs while finding romance in Chandler, Arizona.

The Heart I Rescue (prequel) | (A, E, P)
The Air I Breathe | (A, E, P)
The Shadow I Hide – coming 2024
The Storm I Calm – coming 2025
The Chains I Break – coming 2025

Historical Western Romance

Prescott Pioneers Series:
The series is set in Prescott, Arizona between 1863 - 1870. Follow the lives of the Andersons, Colters, Larsons, Cahills, and Lancasters as they deal with heartache and hope for a new life in Arizona.

A Dream Unfolding | (A, E, P)
A Heart Renewed | (E, P)
A Life Restored | (E, P)
A Hope Revealed | (E, P)
Hidden Prospects | (E, P)

A = Audiobook, E = eBook, P = Paperback

Desert Manna Series:
Follows the lives of three different couples as they trust God through tragedy, heartache, and restoration. Set in Prescott, Arizona between 1871 - 1873.

Beauty for Ashes | (E, P)
Joy for Mourning | (E, P)
Oaks of Justice | (E, P)

Colter Sons Series:
Coming of age stories about Will and Hannah Colter's five sons and their surprise daughter. Set in Prescott and other locations within the Arizona Territory in 1887 - 1906.

The Reluctant Cattleman | (E, P)
The Roaming Adventurer | (E, P)
The Railroad Magnate | (E, P)
The Resourceful Stockman | (E, P)
The Restless Wrangler | (E, P)
The Resilient Bride | (E, P)

Starry Night Novellas:
One starry night, three sisters pray for the man of their dreams. Caty dreams of a godly man who makes beautiful things from wood. Penny's heart belongs to Nathan Cahill. If only he felt the same. Dory longs for a man like her father. Set in Prescott, Arizona in 1886 - 1894.

Caty's Craftsman | (E, P)
Penny's Pursuit | (E, P)
Dory's Desire | (E, P)

A = Audiobook, E = eBook, P = Paperback

She lost everyone...
...her heartache keeps her distant.

Reunited with a bully from her past.

He had a crush on her in high school.

Now they must work together on a new cutting-edge flight control system using her programming skills and his piloting experience.

Can she let go of her resentment to see the man he has become?

As Niki throws herself full tilt into the project, she heads for burn out. Kyle sees his opportunity to get on her good side.

Is rescuing her the key to winning her heart?

You'll love this contemporary Christian romance because of the witty banter and hope for second chances.

Join Niki and Kyle in this sweet enemies-to-sweethearts romance.

Previously released under the title "Nickels".

Available formats: audiobook | ebook | paperback